THE KING OF

THE
KING
OF
INDIA

BY **JABBOUR DOUAIHY**

TRANSLATED BY **PAULA HAYDAR**

Interlink Books

An imprint of Interlink Publishing Group, Inc.
Northampton, Massachusetts

First published in 2022 by

Interlink Books
An imprint of Interlink Publishing Group, Inc.
46 Crosby Street, Northampton, MA 01060
www.interlinkbooks.com

Library of Congress Cataloging-in-Publication data available:
ISBN-13: 978-1-62371-907-4

Printed and bound in the United States of America

This translation is humbly dedicated to the memory of the late Jabbour Douaihy, whose dear soul so sadly "tasted death" before he could experience the joy of seeing it in print.

1

Zakariya Bin Ibrahim Mubarak came back at the start of summer, just as the cherries and goat cheese were coming into season. He came back to his birthplace, Tel Safra, that town situated on a plain seven hundred meters above sea level, where valley and mountain fruits thrive equally well.

In peaceful times, Arab tourists from the Gulf flocked to it. It was home to a public high school that carried the name of a famous vernacular poet who was a native of the town, and to another private school for both girls and boys run by Sister Constance, a nun of the order of the Two Holy Hearts. The town had a police station for the Internal Security Forces, manned by a sergeant and three officers, and a public hospital whose director constantly complained about the lack of medical equipment. It was also home to the ruins of a Roman temple, and the members of the Municipal Council, who ran unopposed in elections, represented all the town's Christian and Druze families equally, with the position of Council President alternating between the two parties.

The people of the town loved to travel because they were a stone's throw from the "international" highway that connected travelers to the Mediterranean Sea. During the twentieth century, they witnessed with their own eyes the flux of outbound travelers by land from Syria or Iraq on their way to Beirut, and the throngs from there in recent times because of the devastation of their countries, all heading to the seaports and airports of the world.

With his departure, Zakariya was carrying on a tradition that had begun centuries before. The first townsperson to set sail did so surreptitiously, dressed as a Muslim woman, carrying a silk abaya and a letter from the great Amir Fakhr al-Din to Cosimo the Second, the Grand Duke of Florence, in which he requested reinforcements of rifles and gold in order to fight off the Ottoman Governor of Damascus. The messenger stayed there; he studied Latin and participated in the translation of *The Old Testament.* He fell head over heels for a woman in the duke's court. He wound up in prison for some unpaid debts and eventually returned, to a hermitage in the Valley of the Monks in north Lebanon, where he wrote a five-volume history of humankind.

The second townsperson was forcefully expelled in the nineteenth century by a scheme devised by the French Consul, along with silk traders from the city of Lyon. He was exiled to Algeria where he wrote letters in which he was the first to call for an Arab Union, though he didn't outline the specifics very clearly. He envisioned a project to extract ore from the red soil mountain near his town, and he might have been the first Christian in those parts to curse France and oppose its policies.

Things continued in that manner during the times of hardship and poverty at the turn of the twentieth century when some young men from the town, and some of the women, too, set out in all directions, and wherever they settled, their motto was that "buying and selling" was sanctioned by God. They were business tycoons who sought to get close to the powerful and influential people. A few of them returned to their town.

The most famous one was a Druze man who'd found that the name Douqan didn't suit him during his time abroad, so he changed it to Jorge. He learned the pharmaceutical arts in Argentina and opened a pharmacy in Tel Safra where he prepared castor oil and ground various seeds and made aphrodisiac potions that they said he learned from the American Indians. He was in high demand and even started setting broken bones and putting on plaster casts. He delivered a woman in emergency childbirth, but he was terror-stricken when the baby came out, and after that he decided to stop getting involved in things that didn't concern him. He was skeptical about the benefits of penicillin, and he would talk to himself in a loud voice while waving his outstretched arms. That earned him the saying that he'd been, "slapped silly by the sea," which stuck with him until he died. That phrase also got applied to others after him who came back from overseas with strange habits, like a woman who'd survived the sinking of the Titanic. She spent long years sitting alone on the balcony of her house smoking Arab tobacco, surrounded by a large clutter of cats. Some nights the neighbors could hear her calling out in her sleep for her husband, whom the guards had barred from climbing aboard the lifeboat with her. She'd say that she was answering him, that she could hear his voice calling her name from out there—where he still was, at the bottom of the ocean.

Zakariya came back, too. He arrived at nightfall, unannounced. He appeared in the doorway of his family's house like a bewildered ghost who'd lost his way. His sister Marta let out a trill of joy. It awakened her sick aunt Raheel, who was asleep in the chair in the living room, reverberated through the town, and then rolled down to the bottom of Hajal Valley. Marta finally got over the shock, only to start pounding her brother's chest with her fists. Then she hugged him and breathed in the smell of him while chiding him, "If I'd run into you in the street, I wouldn't recognize you. Look how skinny you are! Come here! I'll take care of you." Aunt Raheel was sitting exactly where she had been before he left. He kissed her on the head while she laughed. Marta informed him that Raheel had been spending the whole night there during the summer and refused to put on new clothes.

Marta cried tears of joy over Zakariya's arrival and then scolded him for coming back. Then she hugged him all over again and offered to help him unpack his things. But he wouldn't allow it. He carried his suitcases to his parents' room himself. He walked over to the window and pushed against the iron bars, making sure they were sturdy. He opened the big suitcase. He pulled out a metal tube from the bottom of it and inspected it from all angles without opening it, making sure it had survived the long trip. With great care, he also picked up a dark glass bottle packed in his bag that had a cork stopper like a wine bottle and the name "Mary" written on it. He placed it on the night table next to the bed, close to where his head would be. He locked the door with the key and went back to spend the evening with Marta.

He made an effort to smile as she brought him food that he didn't eat. She talked incessantly. His phone rang, so she stopped to let him answer, but he just looked at the screen and ignored the call. She asked him which countries he liked that he thought she should visit. But before he could answer, she told him she'd kept the few letters he'd sent and that she used to read them to their mother over and over again. Suddenly she wanted to know if he had gotten married and if he had children. He didn't answer. He choked up and turned his face away toward Aunt Raheel who had just woken up again. She raised her hands up to the heavens and spoke some incomprehensible words as usual, which Marta translated, having developed an ability to decode her speech after years of companionship. "She says, now that you've come back home, she can die in peace!"

Marta gave back the watch she'd stolen from him before he left, and she told him about some displaced Iraqis who'd stopped in the town after being forced to leave their country and how they were still living there. They were well-mannered, skilled at various trades, and wouldn't accept charity. She talked and talked as though, if she were to stop talking, her silence would force her to face some overwhelming emotions, conflicting emotions that had been awakened by her brother's return and that she wouldn't be able to control. He wrapped his arms around her and hugged her close to him, telling her everything was going to be all right. She felt better. They drank mint tea at midnight. She got sleepy, so Zakariya went into his parents' bedroom and flopped down on their brass bed.

The first night passed. Every time he started to nod off, he would wake up suddenly, feeling he was suffocating. He'd start to tremble and lie awake wide-eyed in the dark, until the light of dawn crept in through the cracks in the window. He was completely exhausted after getting barely an hour's sleep all night.

They spent the whole summer together. She sang *mawwals* about falling in love—something she'd longed for but never got to taste. Then she'd ask him when he was going to leave again, as though encouraging him. He would stick his lower lip out without answering. She would say to her neighbors who came to congratulate her for his return that travel had made her brother silent. She prepared the morning coffee, strong the way she liked it. He would sip it while it was hot, looking out the window, and his eyes would fill with tears whenever he could hear children kicking a ball around and calling out to each other beneath the big walnut tree. Aunt Raheel would scold them sharply, but they didn't care. He kept his passport, his various cards, and his driver's license in the dresser drawer. He wouldn't need them in town. No one here would ask him for his ID. He locked the bedroom door and pushed hard on it making sure it was secure. Marta tried to persuade him not to go out too much or stay out late at night. "I'm not sure why, but I'm worried about you."

He walked toward the town square. The road stretched before him amid the poplar trees and the houses built of chiseled stone. He walked slowly. A morning with a clear sky and bright sun came crashing through his memory. He dodged the nosy newspaper vendor, stopped to flip through the *Daily Star*, and then folded it up, using it to shade his head from the sun as he walked through the narrow streets. He could recognize people from his hometown from their faces, the shape of their heads, the tone of their voices, even if they'd been born after he left. He greeted the fat and garrulous butcher who had inherited his father's trade as well as his vocabulary. He stood for a long time in the doorway of the bakery whose owner still made *qatayef* pancakes with powdered sugar and Arabic bread. She asked him what he would like, so he flashed her an affectionate smile and answered, "Just your good health and well-being."

He waved to people who recognized him after his long absence and asked how he was doing, and to young men who had no idea who this skinny man in the loose-fitting linen suit and white straw hat was who behaved like a tourist even though he wasn't one.

He went with the church endowment agent to the public cemetery. He had never visited the family tomb before. Men there did not visit cemeteries. He and the agent deliberated about the cost to restore the two marble angels that stood on top of it, to have the stone cleaned, and to replace the iron door that had rusted. Zakariya asked about the names of the families around it; neighbors in death are different from neighbors in life.

So many thoughts had filled his mind throughout his time away from there. Thoughts of throwing himself off a high bridge into the water below and ending his life there in the middle of that world, in Paris or New York, not here at the distant ends of the earth. He would wear the gray suit he'd had custom tailored at Stark & Sons at a time when his wallet was bulging with cash. He'd worn it only once, the day one of his flirtatious women friends invited him to a ball at a hotel in the French capital. And he'd wear the Prussian red eagle medal on his chest that he'd bought cheap at a flea market. He would stand on the bridge railing and recite the poem of al-Farazdaq praising Zayn al-Abideen Bin Husayn before surrendering himself to the void and the water.

But in the end, he was swayed by the idea of being laid to rest here among his relatives and townsfolk where he could have a view of a sea that was small but centuries deep. He could lie near the ones who had been murdered, and buried beside the others who were then killed to avenge them. And beside the woman who people said used to get completely naked and dance amid the ruins of the Roman temple with her hair flowing wildly on nights lit by a full moon. Men were terrified of her and wouldn't dare go near the place. He would lie beside his mother

Emily who never tasted the pleasures of the world a single day in her life, motherhood having been one source of her long suffering. And beside his uncle Younis and his sons who believed they had been shortchanged out of their fair share of the family inheritance.

At one o'clock he went to eat by himself at Dulb Café— to save his sister the trouble of preparing lunch. During his time overseas, he cooked all those foods whose aromas he'd carried with him. He introduced the French to *baba ghannouj* and the Americans to stuffed squash and eggplant, but he lost interest in being hospitable and serving food. He started ordering. Straight *arak* not mixed with water and green olives with fennel. Watercress drenched in olive oil and lemon. Dandelion. Lavash flat bread. He set it all up the way he had imagined it while they were serving him on airplanes or in cheap hotels on his way from the United States—foods with lots of color but no flavor. He gazed upon the simple spread. He gazed at the blue-hued mountain. He shut his eyes for a while, then stretched his arms up to the sky before raising his glass—making a toast in response to the restaurant owner who was drinking with his customers— from the table where he sat all by himself.

He went back home and stretched out on the living room sofa near Aunt Raheel, with his hat lowered over his face shading the light, while Marta read to him from her journal a list of all the town's now-extinct shoemakers and tailors, the names of all the water springs, and a page in which she explains why she didn't want to get married. In it she talks about someone she refers to as "the traitor" who asked her without an ounce of shame about her father's inheritance. She told him he'd left them only the house and the orchard, both of which she ceded to her brother. He didn't like what he heard, so he turned his back and walked away. He could walk all the way to hell! She wouldn't divulge his name.

She went on at great length about a lawyer Zakariya knew whom she had liked and who had liked her, but neither one knew how to enter the other's heart, so they got stuck standing at the door until another girl who didn't ask permission to show her feelings stole him away.

She resumed reading from her journal while Zakariya shut his eyes, pretending to take a nap though not sleeping, and opening them whenever Marta stopped reading. He decided to go out and head back to the town square once again. He wandered into the café where the regulars had grown accustomed to his sad face and kind personality. "Hi Zak," they'd call to him, something between endearment and mockery, as they sat down around the round green card table. He followed their chatter for a few minutes, smiling along with their anecdotes. Then he walked past them to sit with a man who was all by himself, a stranger whose accent gave him away when he spoke to the waiter. Zakariya's accent was also outdated. He'd taken it away with him for decades and preserved it just as it was. He introduced himself and asked if he could sit down.

"Where are you from?" he asked the man.

The man waved his hand vaguely toward the east as if tired of answering that question. A long silence ensued between them, so Zakariya started to get up, not wanting to annoy the stranger, but then the latter suddenly started talking. He was retelling the story that made people take interest in him.

"Mosul fell, and we woke up two days later to some noise and commotion. We found a man wearing a keffiyeh and *agal*

15

standing on the roof of the Municipality Building. He fired a round of bullets from his machine gun to draw the attention of the townspeople before urging them to leave their houses at once and head north, toward the Kurdish villages."

The Iraqi rubbed his hands together incessantly, turning his skin red whenever recent memories came crowding in. He was quiet for a bit before going on.

"My mother went crazy. She started yelling incomprehensible things as if a strange language had suddenly been awakened inside her. A language whose sounds were familiar to us, but which we couldn't understand, not a single word. Then she started kissing the walls, the windows, and the furniture. She refused to take anything with her. My nephew went around taking pictures of everything with his phone: the rooms, the beds, the trees, the road. Every nook and cranny. He even took pictures of the clouds over our houses. We were crammed into cars. The young men were forced to sit on the car tops. We left in one last convoy with nothing but our clothes and our money. They arrived hours later. They burned down our town, and we were all scattered—me, my brothers, and our families. We've come to you here, but we won't stay long. We're just waiting for our visas to Canada. We were promised we would get them in three months."

Zakariya's phone rang. He glanced at the screen and ignored the call.

"Why don't you stay here with us?"

"We don't want to get stung twice. We want our children to grow up in a stable country. It's cold there, that's true, but it's stable."

Zakariya nearly told the Iraqi the story of his long years away from his homeland in "stable" countries and his decision to come back for good to his birthplace, but he couldn't see the point in talking about it. He wished the man luck and left.

In the afternoon, he headed for Mahmoudiya Orchard—a half-hour walk. He had come there to look into the distant horizon, to the pages of his life receding beyond the sea. And on a beautiful fall day, when the leaves had started turning yellow and red, a group of hikers spotted him from a distance, sitting up in his linen suit like someone who had been relaxing there and then dozed off. When they came closer, they saw the big red blotch of blood staining the white of his suit. A single bullet to the heart had killed him!

2

The body was discovered by a group from the Ancient Paths Club—an organization established, according to its bylaws, "for the sake of nurturing a passion for walking in nature, for discovering its fruits and its rocks, the eagles and the foxes, and finding beneath every stone a story and over every hill a glorious achievement." The hikers discovered Zakariya Mubarak there on the hillside at five o'clock on Sunday afternoon. They had been at a loss as to which way to go after their GPS failed to guide them to the mule path leading to the other side of the valley, when one of them spotted Zakariya in the distance. There he sat, lounging in the shade of a crab apple tree—the kind that produces small pale fruits that birds peck away at the moment they ripen, and passersby avoid eating.

The hiker whistled through two fingers to alert his companions. Believing the man was enjoying a nap, they called out to him a few times in the hope that he could help them find their way, but he didn't turn his head. They walked over and discovered he was dead. The two young women in the group shrieked in unison. His eyes were wide open and directed up at the blue sky adorned with a bashful cloud, perhaps not believing what just happened. His face expressed pain, but most likely he only felt the start of that pain and would never taste its end, because midway through his suffering he died. The straw hat hadn't fallen to the ground even though his head was tilted back. His mouth gaped open, and he had drooled a little before surrendering to eternity. He was sitting in his blood, which had stained his clothes as it flowed, leaving a few scattered spots that were still dark red, an indication that he hadn't been dead for long. With his right arm he had covered the hole that had been torn through his chest, in a belated defensive motion or as an attempt to press down on the source of the pain.

A young man from the group of hikers who was a medical student went close and felt Zakariya's neck, searching for the carotid artery rather than taking his pulse at his wrist. He moved near Zakariya's mouth and checked his breathing before pronouncing him dead to the others by means of a sideways hand motion. Everyone bowed their heads in silence. Then, two of them dialed the numbers for rescue and emergency services, and they all waited near Zakariya for half an hour. One of the young women burst into a fit of hysterical laughter that was punctuated with intermittent sobs.

The white Nissan Patrol arrived from the town police station with the sergeant and driver on board. It had sent a cloud of dust rising up behind it as it traversed from the asphalt onto the dirt road leading to the overlook at the edge of the pine grove. The police station telephone had rung at 4:50 p.m. informing the police a dead body had been discovered there, but the caller refused to identify himself. Sometimes people who'd had some experience dealing with security forces would decline to give their names in such circumstances to avoid being held for questioning and having their time wasted serving as witnesses before a judge if the matter ended up in court. The motor of the outdated four-wheel drive vehicle—which was the station's only vehicle—wouldn't start until after fifteen minutes of attempts and curses from the sergeant who, on each try, begged God to speed up the passing of the few months separating him from retirement.

As soon as he got out of the vehicle, reeking of cheap whiskey, his face tensed up, in confirmation of what he had been told about the scary look on the dead man's face. In an accusing tone, he asked the people gathered around the body if they had called to report it to the police. They said they called 112 and the Red Cross. Then a cell phone started ringing. The people who had cell phones with a similar ring tone checked to see if it was their phone ringing. No one's. They exchanged glances with each other, realizing it belonged to the dead man. None of the bystanders volunteered to search for the phone. The entire group—all ten members of the hiking club, plus the two police officers—stood still, listening to the intermittent ringing until it finally died out.

The sergeant didn't recognize the dead man, and neither did his colleague, despite their having served in the town for two years. He told the hikers to leave, attaching to his request a hand gesture indicating they should hurry up and be gone from the place. He felt there was no need to drive them down to the police station, take their statements, and deal with all of them after finding out they were strangers to the town who had only come there to pursue their hobby. So, they took off, dumbfounded, endeavoring to reach their next stop before nightfall.

The medical student walked along slowly, trailing behind his companions. He looked back and stopped hesitantly as though he wanted to return to the area around the crab apple tree. He wanted to tell the two police officers that he had seen a gun tossed in the brush a few meters from the corpse. Only he had seen it because he was the only one to go close to the body. It was a Glock, a recent model, a Glock 17.

He worried that divulging this information might hold up the whole group while he gave his statement. So when his friends noticed him lagging behind them and called out to him insistently, he decided it was best to catch up with the other hikers who had already gone over the slope and disappeared from view. The young man would often think back on the gravity of what he had done, but he wouldn't dare change his decision to cover it up, because that would put him personally under suspicion, so he wrestled with his conscience and tried his best to forget. What helped him move on was that he hadn't told anyone—not even his hiking buddies—about seeing the gun.

Afterward, the sergeant phoned the deputy back at the station and asked him to send the medical examiner over at once, before it got dark, and to send an ambulance, and to inform the Mount Lebanon Prosecutor that there'd been a homicide on the outskirts of the town of Tel Safra at five o'clock p.m. Then he took that back and without any supporting evidence changed the time to "Four…fifteen." When the deputy officer at the station asked for ID on the victim for his report, the sergeant asked him to hold on while the dead man's pockets were searched. It wasn't easy for the driver, who was getting sick and tired of his commander's orders and was rattled by the sight of the dead man swimming in a pool of his own blood, to reach into the dead man's trousers and jacket. Using his fingertips, he was finally able to extract a black leather wallet from the inner pocket of his jacket. All he found in the remaining pockets was a bedroom key and a cell phone.

From the wallet the sergeant pulled out some US dollars, some Lebanese currency, some pictures, and some handwritten letters, some of which were in a small child's handwriting, plus a piece of paper that had numerous official stamps on it. All the papers were written in English or French. He didn't find an ID card. It was getting dark, and the sergeant was having a hard time making out the writing, and he was far from being an expert on foreign languages, so he tried again to sound out bits and pieces, revealing his annoyance and bad mood. He put the money and the papers back inside the wallet and tried to resume his phone conversation, only to discover that the deputy had gotten tired of waiting and hung up. He called him back, swore at him right and left, and finally informed him that they had found a body, identity unknown. He was dressed in a white suit and was wearing a hat ...end of story. The sergeant said, "end of story."

He and the driver waited there, trying not to look at the corpse. They knew they had to preserve the crime scene as much as possible. The sergeant placed Zakariya's belongings in an envelope. He picked up the cell phone, and when it rang again, he recoiled in fear and dropped it on the ground, cutting off the call.

They stood there a long time with the sun at the edge of the sea's horizon. When the driver stepped away to go relieve himself behind the trees, the sergeant scoped the area with his eyes before bending over a mass of thorns and easily pulling out the Glock that he'd spotted the moment they arrived. He tucked it into his pocket. It weighed no more than half a kilogram. The price of that Austrian-made pistol on the Lebanese black market was equivalent to three whole months' salary for the sergeant.

The Red Cross ambulance arrived at 5:30, lights flashing, the intermittent siren tearing through the autumn sky. A short young man with a beard came out of the vehicle along with a skinny red-headed young woman, at whom the sergeant cast a cryptic glance. They took a look around, tensing up a bit when they spotted Zakariya Mubarak lifeless and covered in blood, and then waited with the officers. The sergeant kept silent, imposing his prestige on everyone, while the two ambulance medics sat on the ground, drawing lines in the dirt with sticks and whispering about matters that did not appear to have anything to do with the crime that they had been called to at sundown in Tel Safra.

The medical examiner arrived at around seven in his own car. He showed no sign of alarm, didn't ask a single question, and didn't say hello. The first-aid workers winked at each other about his fake hair. He asked for a flashlight, so the young woman brought one from the ambulance and shined it on the dead man while the doctor knelt over him. Finally, he asked who found the body, and the sergeant volunteered an answer, claiming that he and his assistant had been the first to arrive on the crime scene after receiving a call at the station, not paying the least bit of attention to the driver glaring at him disapprovingly for his lie. The doctor tugged at the skin below the dead man's eye to examine the white of his eyes. He moved on to the neck, felt it, and from there to the fingers and nails and asked the woman to bring the light closer. He moved the dead man's arm off his chest and began inspecting the hole made by the bullet. He shook his head as though he'd discovered something important. Suddenly he turned to the sergeant. "Did you find a gun near the body?"

He quickly answered in the negative. The medical examiner shrugged his shoulders and curled his lips. Maybe he had doubts about what he'd deduced concerning the crime, or maybe he didn't believe the sergeant.

He'd come down with an out-of-season cold and was badly congested. He kept sneezing and blowing his nose. He asked the male paramedic to help him sit the body up so he could examine the exit wound caused by the bullet. Then he asked the young woman to shine the flashlight in the area around the victim. He found the bullet that had pierced the man's body, handed it over to the sergeant, and warned him not to lose it. He knew the sergeant from previous incidents. He turned to take another look around the body when the flashlight the woman was holding went out. The battery had died. The medical examiner told the two paramedics to take the body to the town hospital and grumbled that he wasn't going to write his report in the dark. He left the crime scene coughing and sneezing, without saying goodbye and without even asking about the victim's identity.

The driver helped the two medics move the body onto the stretcher. Then he climbed into the jeep and went back to the station accompanied by the sergeant who was feeling pessimistic about this crime as he went over it in his mind, just like the medical student, wondering what it meant that there was a pistol near the victim and why the medical examiner had asked about finding a gun. His decision to resume swigging his whiskey didn't help him to see things clearly.

The ambulance pulled into the front entrance to the town hospital's Emergency Department without sounding the siren. A silent quarrel arose between the two male nurses on duty there about which of them could pass the burden of dealing with the incoming patient onto the other, until, upon inspecting his pitiful condition and detecting putrid odors emanating from him, they became convinced that one nurse would not be able to do the job by himself. They helped each other remove Zakariya's clothing and found a picture of a little girl who couldn't be more than five years old sewn inside his shirt near his heart. One of the nurses looked at it carefully: a pretty face, blond hair, sparkling eyes, full of intelligence and life. He glanced randomly at the dead man's face, looking for some resemblance which he thought he found, and then he tucked the picture into his jacket pocket. They cleaned off the corpse and washed it while awaiting instructions from the medical examiner. At that public hospital that had been built with funding from a gift from the Italian government, no one recognized Zakariya either. A thick gray blanket resembling an army blanket was laid over him before he was rolled into the mortuary refrigerator.

At first, news spread that the victim was a stranger to the town who might have been passing through or had come from a nearby village. Then a young nurse who came in for her nightshift recognized his clothing and his hat and his brown and white shoes that were piled up on the floor of the corridor next to the mortuary refrigerator. She told the director of the hospital that the dead man was her parents' neighbor, Zakariya Mubarak, who had recently returned to his homeland from abroad after a very long absence. He had a sister named Marta who should be notified. The director phoned her at home and asked her to come in because her brother had "lost his footing in the pine grove" and had been taken to the hospital. Marta, who was watching television while waiting for Zakariya to get home so they could share the light dinner she'd prepared, sensed the matter was more serious than the director let on. She locked the door with the key on her way out so her aunt wouldn't think about following her and rushed into town tearful and angry. Her neighbor the nurse gave her a big hug. Marta knew for sure that Zakariya was dead.

They went with her to identify him. She cried out and then she kissed him on the forehead. He was completely naked. She saw the bullet hole in his chest. They tried to console her. The male nurse handed her the picture of the little girl and told her it was all they found on her brother. Amid the flood of tears, she asked who that was in the picture. He said he didn't know, and she took the picture from him.

Marta sat in the emergency room, sobbing, and saying she had been expecting this. He had phoned her several times telling her he wanted to come back, and every time, her attempts to dissuade him had failed. "This is my hometown," she said, mimicking his accent. "This is my home. I want to go out in the morning to sit on the wooden bench beneath the walnut tree."

She cut him off, telling him there was no bench in the shade of the tree anymore. Some children had tampered with it and then they broke it apart and burned the wood on Transfiguration Sunday. He scoffed at her, "I want to sit at the front door of the house so I can be friendly with the passersby and invite them in for coffee. I want to gaze into the distance at night and see the headlights of the cars making their way down to Beirut."

She wept as she spoke. She didn't believe that he'd come back just because he missed fried eggs with *kishk* and bitter green olives—the ones from the first harvest—and goat cheese. He adored goat cheese. He'd eat some every day if only a single bite. He liked to eat it with watermelon, or with pear preserves dipped in sugar, and especially with grapes. He said his grandfather taught him to eat goat cheese with sweet grapes. He didn't eat much, but despite that he'd roamed the whole world and then come back for the goat cheese. She went on at length in a calm voice before breaking down in tears. She spoke in the direction of where her brother was in the mortuary refrigerator in the adjoining room. "Stubborn. You didn't believe me. I warned you they would kill you and that's what they did."

No one at the hospital asked who "they" were. At home, she spoke in her usual manner to a friend who had accompanied her to the house and some other women who'd come over to try to calm her down as she wept for Zakariya and for herself. She was all alone once again in that big house. Alone with Raheel—who had one foot in the grave. They all died. When she left the hospital, they didn't give her the key to her brother's room so she could bring him some clothes. His papers and his phone and everything they'd found in his pockets had been taken into custody by the sergeant. He said they were crime scene evidence.

"What am I supposed to do now? Break the door down?"

She'd weep for herself and then go back to her brother. She'd lament his good heart and his generosity and good character. Then she'd burst into tears all over again. He'd said once that he came back so he could spend the rest of his years among family. Suddenly she whispered between her sobs that it was his family who killed him. She'd quiet down and then raise her voice to the point of screaming.

"Yes! His cousins threatened me, and they threatened him. They said they weren't going to flex their muscles at a woman. They were going to wait for him to return. I told him and I warned him, but he didn't care."

She continued her questions.

"What fault is it of ours, the children of Ibrahim Mubarak? Let them ask their grandfather Jibrail. He was the one who wanted it that way. Let them ask their great-grandmother Philomena who built this house with her own money and bought Mahmoudiya

Orchard with her own money and bequeathed them both to whomever she wished."

She paused for a moment before firing off her final judgment.

"It was our great-grandmother Philomena who got us here."

3

Philomena's life changed in the blink of an eye. One morning, her husband tucked his pruning shears into his cummerbund and told her not to expect him for lunch. He stood at the door, and, out of habit, he turned to take a good look at her sitting there with her protruding belly. That was the only tender look that he cast her way their entire life together. He was stingy with words. He never complained a single day about lacking anything or having any pain. She had seen some dark red blood on his white underwear but didn't ask him about it. From time to time, he would let out a heavy sigh while looking up at the ceiling. But she never suspected for a single moment that he would turn and leave her in her seventh month of pregnancy. But out the door he stepped. Some wood gatherers from Tel Safra saw him walking down to the overlook at the edge of the pine grove and then all trace of him was lost. The world swallowed him up.

She was blessed with a baby boy on the Feast of Annunciation, so she named him Jibrail. She held off on baptizing him in the hope that his father would reappear. When he started walking on his own, she pinned all her hopes on taking her own journey and left him in the care of her sister Katarina.

She was compelled by need, and by the despair accumulating all around her, and by the hope of finding her husband Yusuf Mubarak. People told her that her son wouldn't recognize her when she returned and that it would be better to postpone her travels until he'd gotten bigger and stronger. But, afraid she would lose her nerve, she refused to change her mind. The last day, a relative of hers broke her promise to go with her, as she was frightened by all the talk she'd heard about the perils of traveling. Philomena had enough money to cover the cost of the outbound sea voyage plus a few necessities, but nothing for the return trip. She took a deep breath and said to herself, "No one is for anyone in this world," and walked on.

She got seasick after an hour on the ship. Her ears started ringing, and she was sweating so profusely that she thought she would die there suspended between the sky and the water, with the Lebanese mountain peaks still in view. Some experienced passengers advised her to drink some ginger juice which helped settle her stomach, and she deboarded in Marseille. She heard a bell ring out at the train station announcing an incoming train, so she knelt to the ground amid all the travelers and made the sign of the cross, for she'd imagined that they were bringing Holy Communion to some sick person on his death bed, as often happened in her village. A Jewish salesman told her to look after her appearance and told her she should buy new shoes to ease her entry into New York. Before saying goodbye, he said to her, "Bathe often, for you are very beautiful and luck is going to smile upon you."

She didn't buy shoes. Instead, she chose a wool coat that complimented her black eyes, and while on the ship *La Rochelle*

She remembered the Frenchman Monsieur Lagrange whom the mulatto sailor had told her to go see as a reward for their sweet encounter. She found him in Brooklyn—an old man whose wife had died a few weeks earlier. He welcomed her, telling himself that fate had sent him this radiant face. They communicated with each other using what they could of sounds and hand gestures and facial expressions, and the next morning, she pulled a heavy sack out from her belongings, opened it in front of the man, and succeeded with gestures toward the distant east and kneeling and kissing the ground to convey to him that she had brought with her some soil from Jerusalem. He gaped in awe as he inspected a handful of it and started clapping for joy. He realized she was as clever as she was beautiful and began cutting and sewing little hemp sacks with her that they filled with the soil. He wrote "Jerusalem" on them in English. That was not all Philomena had in store. She picked up a piece of wood, one of the logs Lagrange collected for the wood stove inside his house and told him to cut it up into little slivers. Then she started putting them into other sacks as she acted out the crucifixion, moaning and stretching her arms outward. He understood what she meant while his admiration for her grew. He wrote on the sacks "Wood from the Holy Cross." She also had procured copies of the New Testament in Arabic that she found among the wares of a merchant coming from Haifa that she would say were written in Jesus Christ's mother tongue. Lagrange dressed her up in what he thought was the typical garb of a Palestinian woman, flung a white scarf over her head, and tied a big brass cross around her neck. He taught her how to recognize Abraham Lincoln by his thick beard on the one-dollar bill, and Thomas Jefferson with the white hair on the two-dollar bill. He sent her to an Evangelical group that was very dedicated to its faith, the "Seventh Day Adventists," who resided in one of the city's suburbs. She started going around to their houses. She'd knock at the door while repeating without pause the words, "Jesus, Holy Cross, Bible, Jerusalem," that the Frenchman had taught her to say.

Business boomed. She added some embroidery and small rugs to the goods she carried on her shoulders. The farmers shooed her away from their homes. Guard dogs barked in her face. Her merchandise was stolen but the robbers didn't get to the money she kept tucked between her breasts. Her English improved, and she kept up acquaintance with people from her country so she could check on her son's well-being whenever newcomers arrived from her town or neighboring towns. She met a man who could send money back to the old country, and so she sent letters to her son and some dollars to her sister for compensation, half of which the man kept as his fee. On one of her excursions to the nearby countryside, a bearded Dutchman bought some sacks of "wood from the holy cross" which she saw him toss into the foundations of a house he was just starting to build—as protection for the house and its inhabitants from all forms of evil.

She spent years selling her goods, returning in the evening to put the day's earnings in the care of Monsieur Lagrange who no longer kept anything secret from her. It wasn't long before he passed away after filling the house with his coughing fits from a severe chest cold. He didn't leave the world before instructing Philomena to take and enjoy everything he owned, repeatedly assuring her that he had no relatives in New York nor in his birthplace Saint-Paul-de-Vence in southern France. She would kneel beside his bed, praying for him to recover, but he would stop her and tell her to get up because he didn't believe in such superstitions.

His suspicions came true. Sometime after his death, after a period of forty days which Philomena spent dressed in black mourning clothes, a young man showed up claiming, in French, that he was Lagrange's nephew. So, she asked him in English how many fingers the deceased had on his left hand. "Four," he answered, to which she responded, "No. Five. And if you come back here, I'll go to the police and have you put in jail." He left and never came back. The day she heard a newspaper boy running by, waving a copy of *The Evening World* and shouting that the war was over, she realized that the time had come for her to return to her son. She sold everything she could, packed up what could be packed up, and waited for the "La Rochelle" to dock in New York Harbor so she could get back on board under a good omen. She asked about her sailor and the captain told her that he had joined the French navy and was killed in the attack on the Dardanelles Strait. She also remembered the violin player. She realized how much her heart had hardened between the two voyages.

————

She stayed as a guest of her sister Katarina. The house was crammed with curious onlookers getting a good look at the immigrant who had come back from abroad with a gilded handbag and a fancy hat on her head that looked like the one worn by the wife of the French general with the amputated hand who had recently come to inspect the mountain villages. They found her sitting with her arms wrapped around her son. He kept his gaze fixed on her, inspecting her nose and the wrinkles on her face, unbuckling the scarab brooch on the collar of her jacket, and fiddling with her bracelets.

He got confused. His entire childhood he had called his aunt "mama" and the cousin with whom he shared a bed every night, "brother." His aunt never corrected him, fearing that his mother might never come back, just like his father. But he clung to her the moment his aunt called to him with jubilation saying, "Your mother has returned!"

Philomena told the crowd about the Statue of Liberty and described for them the shape of the Chinese people's eyes and the Black people's noses. She showed them some postcards depicting the Brooklyn Bridge suspended in the air and women riding on elephants in the public park. She asked a couple of men to help drag her trunk into the middle of the parlor. She removed all the strappings from it and then opened the locks just as the room became crowded with villagers.

First, she brought out the wall clock and stood it up on the table. She wound the spring with the key and told everyone to be quiet so they could hear it tick and watch the pendulum swing. She started teaching them how to read the time. She would advance the hands and quiz the villagers, who up until then had been content with sunrise and sunset. After that, she took out a box containing a dozen coffee cups with saucers that had a Japanese design of flowers and birds, a portion of which still remained in the Mubarak family household a hundred years later. She followed that with a coffee grinder and a small accordion and a magnifying glass that she positioned beneath the sun's rays and aimed at a newspaper causing it to burn. She handed out little packets of aspirin powder, telling them they should dissolve it in water and drink it to be relieved of headaches, joint pain, and colds. She gave the women some Nile soap to add to the laundry water. For the finale she had a His Master's Voice gramophone with the dog sitting on his hind legs looking at the horn. She cranked it and out came the voice of Claudia Muzio in the role of Desdemona in the opera *Otello*. Everyone was astonished. Some of the simpler folk among them believed they were in the company of a sorceress and remained suspicious of her long after she took up residence with them.

Her plan was plain and simple: build a house for her son and then find him a wife as soon as he started shaving. She sought out the most skilled builders. She intervened if one of them brought back a stone that had not been chiseled properly, and she would spend the whole day sitting in the shade of a tree watching the excavation work. She would tell the workers to deepen the foundations and raise the ceilings high. "No one is better than anyone," she'd say, mentioning the socially prominent people who erected lofty houses. And like the few other families who could afford it, she built one storey with arches, and another covered with red tiles that composed the main hall with its painted ceiling and adjoining rooms connected on every side. She paid for the labor and materials in cash. She insisted on red porphyry stone and *qitran* wood, and she oversaw the fortification of the red rooftiles and the interlocking placement of them, one by one.

The construction of the house took two years, and an entire year was spent customizing the furniture and having it made. Philomena would go down to the carpenters' souq in Beirut to order the beds. She had precise designs in mind for the chairs and sofas, and oversaw upholstering them. As she made her color choices, she always pictured in her mind those houses she'd been inside in the outskirts of New York while selling Jerusalem soil. The tablecloths appealed to her with their red and white squares, as did the sheer curtains, the rocking chairs, and the kitchen cabinets that stored wine glasses and fancy tea sets on their shelves. She put the finishing touches on the house in the most perfect manner. She planted walnut trees all around it and moved in with her son.

38

She "reacclimated" herself—never left the quarter, socialized with the women, drank coffee with them and asked about the "news" if ever they neglected to share their slanderous gossip. Her appearance deteriorated, and she went gray and got fat. Nothing remained of her voyage to America but a few words in English that slipped from her tongue if she had trouble remembering what something was called in Arabic. But after many years, she brought out a fancy gown made of blue satin with a silk scarf that she had gotten from abroad. She wore it on her son Jibrail's wedding day, having saved it specially for that occasion. It was a celebration in which the mother of the groom managed to retrieve one last fleeting glimpse of her beauty and femininity. She chose her son's bride herself after lengthy inquiries. She sat her down to tell her about men and their needs. Then she chose to move her bedroom to the cellar, leaving the entire upper floor to her son and his wife.

After achieving her goal of building a house and marrying off her son, and also purchasing a big orchard—Al-Mahmoudiya—on the mountain slope at the overlook at the edge of the pine grove, Philomena's health deteriorated, and she became bedridden. One day when she heard her son's footsteps going up the stairs, she called to him in a feeble voice from the cellar and asked him to shut the door and come to her bedside. She whispered to him that she was going to die on Sunday. She urged him to look after his aunt Katarina just as she had looked after him while she was away. Then she gave him a sealed letter and made him promise not to open it or read it until a year after her death. She said it contained an important secret and under no circumstances whatsoever was it to fall into the hands of any other person but him.

She actually died on Sunday evening, and Jibrail did not wait long. He opened the letter before they shut the door to *gold English pounds in its foundation. Digging into the base of the house to get at the gold will cause it to collapse, so I advise against doing so. Do not tell this secret to anyone except your eldest son and he his eldest son. Take care of your aunt and your cousin just as they took care of you and remember your mother fondly and pray for her.*

When the bookstore owner finished reading it, Jibrail thanked him profusely and nearly hugged him before heading out the door on his way back to his hometown with a big smile on his face after having his wishes come true in a most perfect way, forgetting all about the letter that the bookstore owner was still holding in his hands…

without having to do strenuous work, as a wanderer in this world, fabricating money-making schemes with whatever things came his way. He took ownership of a fully equipped printing press and then exchanged it after a time for a shipment of military uniforms that he sold to the Australian army that had set up a military base in the area. Or the following year he'd bought a herd of goats and then hastened to get rid of them after hearing reports that the goat herder was stealing goats from him and selling them to butchers in the village. They were deals that mostly ended in losses whose only value was that they gave the impression he was merely making a living and trying to provide for his family while concealing his true work as a money lender offering reasonable interest rates.

He hung the picture of Philomena wearing an embroidered headscarf and holding a small book in her hand—a copy of the *New Testament* that she'd found in the studio where she posed for the photographer in New York. Her face was beautiful, but she had a tense expression. Photographers didn't tell their subjects to smile in those days. He found no trace of his father, and Philomena stopped remembering any of her husband's traits. She forgot him, intentionally forgot him, as a punishment for leaving her. Jibrail grew fond of believing that his father was an adventurer who loved a challenge. He imagined lands at the ends of the earth, beneath a burning sun, that his father would have traveled to and settled down in, and rugged roads and jungles that he trekked through. And one time when a friend took him to see the movie *Gone with the Wind*, he modified his aspirations concerning his father and concocted the idea that his father resembled the actor Clark Gable. And why not? Maybe he was Clark Gable himself. Yes, his father had gone to America and worked in cinema. He'd taken a stage name and there he was right there on the screen. Secretly, Jibrail went back to the city to see the movie three or four times in one month. And he didn't miss any subsequent Clark Gable films with Claudette Colbert or Heidi Lamarr. But always his greatest joy was watching the good-bye embrace scenes between Rhett Butler and Scarlett O'Hara, as though he had a hand in and shared a family inheritance of this passionate love story. Jibrail was good-looking, too, or so he imagined. He tried to grow a thin moustache like Clark Gable to complete the picture, but he didn't know how to trim it the right way when shaving in the morning, so he got rid of it.

He was weak-willed when it came to women. Vulgar. He never passed up an opportunity to hit on anyone he could grab, to compensate himself for having been deprived of bachelor-hood. His wife said that he didn't spare any random woman who came walking down the street, or even the tattooed Bedouin women, the fortune tellers, or the olive pickers. She'd tell the story, powerless before his transgressions, about a woman from the Beqaa who'd come knocking at her door one day with a baby in her arms asking to speak to him in private, to tell him that the baby she was holding was his son. The woman reminded him how he'd chased her one time to Damascus, and she had never been with another man and hadn't gone near her husband who'd been sick for years. He gave her some money and sent her on her way. She came back another time, so he told her to give him the boy if he was his son. He tried to tear the boy from her arms, so she ran off, screaming in fear, and never came back.

Words were the only weapon available to his wife who simply couldn't fix him. "If only you'd take a trip like your father and never come back, it would be a perfect world!"

When he insisted on her giving him sons, she mocked him. "If you know how sons are made, then don't hesitate. And why

45

would God give us a boy anyway, as a punishment to us? A boy just like you or your father?"

After four years of marriage, she gave him a son. During that time, the world nearly fell apart between them, tumbling into a bottomless pit of loud accusations and curses about what would happen if his suspicions that his wife was barren turned out to be true. She gave birth to the baby, but her milk didn't come, so he found a nursing mother in a neighboring village and brought her back with him, carrying the woman's baby in his arms, and housed her and her family in the cellar. He insisted on making sure she ate well, and he'd bring his son Ibrahim to her himself several times a day. He'd sit beside the woman as she gave her breast to the infant. He kept her in the house, providing all her needs and her family's needs despite his son having grown much older. When the woman left and went back to her village, she was pregnant again, and when her son became a young man, many saw a striking resemblance to Jibrail Mubarak from the town of Tel Safra.

His wife got pregnant six times, but life had fated for only two boys and a girl to survive, the physical disparity among them showing up early. The youngest, Younis, had light skin and light-colored eyes. Jibrail attributed his beauty to himself of course. And the oldest, Ibrahim, the father of Zakariya and Marta, had a dark complexion and slender physique. The sister was ill. They named her Raheel. Her nerves were damaged and the electrical activity in her brain was disturbed, so said the French-educated doctor before asking them about a family history of such cases, while the father glared accusingly at his wife. When they told the doctor how Raheel would hit her head against the wall during her fits, he advised them never to leave her unattended as she was capable of hurting herself, or others.

The mother bore the cross of her daughter, refusing to admit her to the asylum. When the girl grew up, she took up sitting on the sofa in the main room of the house with a wool blanket pulled up over her. She would glare at people who came in or out of the house or she'd spew out incomprehensible words at them. Her mother continued to hand feed her and sing lullabies to calm her and rock her to sleep in her arms. She went to the toilet by herself, but her mother forbade her to lock the bathroom door from inside. The father secretly wept two or three times when it became clear that his daughter's illness could not be cured. He looked up to the heavens repeating, "Where did we get this electricity from, my God?"

And he also continued trying to find precedents among his wife's family members, hoping to find an explanation that could put him at ease, before taking on the worries of the world once again.

He was kept busy by the orchard that his mother had bought for him and that everyone envied him for because of its red soil and terraced slope. He thought about developing it or leasing it out, but he discovered that the land was locked in without a road easement connected to it, so he put it off in order to profit from his other easier business dealings. Women kept him busy as usual, too, but not for long this time because he had to undergo surgery to correct his enlarged prostate. His sex drive diminished after that, and he started fuming and railing at the doctors for prescribing medications that made him lose his desire for women. One of the things that came as a result of that was his attempts to get closer to his wife and a bubbling of affection for her. She turned away from him one day and blew up in his face with what he might have expected from her bitter tongue—that she wasn't running a nursing home. But after those hurtful words (something she'd inherited from her father about whom was said, "If he says hi, he'll make you cry"), she was a model wife. A good heart and distributor of motherly emotions in equal measure.

The borrowers kept him busy writing promissory notes in exchange for "miscellaneous goods"—camouflage for the actual interest. His two sons occupied him, or more precisely the younger Younis occupied him. The eldest was obedient and went in whichever direction his father nudged him. He attended boarding school with the Capuchin friars and became proficient in Latin. He memorized countless poems in Arabic and French that he continued to quote up until his death. If there was some mention of the bitter cold of Russia, he would recite for everyone around some verses from Victor Hugo about the defeat of Napoleon I at the doors of Moscow during the bitterly cold winter. And in the face of life's trials and tribulations, he would spout off lines from Abu al-Alaa' al-Maarri.

Younis was antagonistic from childhood. He would leave the house at the first shriek from his sister Raheel having one of her nervous fits. He'd take off with some of his school friends on sunny days and make fun of his diligent older brother whose cheeks would turn red with embarrassment if one of the girls from the town spoke to him. He, on the other hand, went early down the same path as his father, prowling for the opposite sex. But Jibrail wanted a different life for him, and it was unknown from where he'd been struck with that conviction of his that made him repeat his motto at every occasion: "I believe in education." The day he repeated it for the thousandth time in front of Younis, Younis asked, "Then why didn't you go to school?" That led to a quarrel between them that Jibrail ended with a harsh slap across Younis' cheek. After that, Younis took off and didn't come back for a whole week. He started swindling his father, exchanging his good behavior for money that he'd spend haphazardly. He'd head to the Beirut cabarets while Jibrail scolded him, "You pay money to get women? I never paid a single piaster"—lying, of course—"for all the women I enjoyed, and there were a lot of them." Jibrail continued to give him money with constant reluctance and vehemence until the day when his son bought a red and white Chevrolet Corvette direct from the United States and shoved the responsibility of paying the installments to the dealership onto his father after a new fight broke out between them in which Younis tried to hit his father back. Jibrail had no alternative but to hurry in a manner that surprised everyone, Younis included, to pay off the car completely without a word of complaint. From that day on, he no longer refused his youngest son any request and even opened up an account for him in one of the banks from which he could withdraw whatever amount he wanted, and that at a time when he was being tightfisted with Ibrahim who never asked for anything beyond necessities.

Time passed and Jibrail felt weak and started having heart palpitations, so he got scared and kept to the house. Something he said to one of his friends got spread around, which was that his forced abstinence from women was going to be the end of him. He insisted on having a final photograph taken. He sent for the photographer who had recently taken up residence in town. The photographer picked up the wooden model of a young woman dressed in beachwear, the one smiling and waving on the new "Ektachrome" film, and tossed her inside the studio in case someone tried to break in while he was away. He slung the camera over his shoulder, along with the round electric flash. He locked the door with two turns of the key and left, followed by some children who whistled to whichever of their buddies had lagged behind, increasing in number as they moved through the

49

At dusk that day, and when the house had emptied of all the visitors, Jibrail took advantage of the absence of his son Younis—the only one who hadn't shown up to that gathering—and his wife's having gone into the kitchen to do the dishes, to ask his eldest son Ibrahim to come closer to him there where he was stretched out on the sofa. He looked over to check on Raheel and found her hiding her head as usual under the blankets, so he wasn't concerned about her presence, and began to tell Ibrahim the details of his grandmother's will just as the Bliss Street bookstore owner in Beirut had translated for him. When he reached the part about the fortune of gold buried in the house's foundations, Raheel had a sudden severe coughing fit that made her pull the cover off her face and sit up to catch her breath. Her father stopped talking until she resumed her previous position. Jibrail finished relating Philomena's wishes and added a few clauses that suited him. He didn't get any response from his son other than some doubtful smiles, but, trying to please him, Ibrahim asked his father, "How much is an English gold pound worth?"

Jibrail replied that the value varied, but it was worth more than the Ottoman lira and there was a higher demand for it. He pressed upon him the importance of keeping the matter a secret, especially from his brother Younis, because he didn't trust his excessive spending and lust for money. Ibrahim laughed as he imagined his brother digging into the bottom floor of the house causing it to come crashing down over their heads.

Ibrahim was somewhere else, immersed in reading Frederick Engels' *The Origin of the Family, Private Property, and the State*, so he placed his grandmother Philomena's gold in the same category as his father's story and with the passing of time forgot all about it. The latter had topped off his tall stories concerning *Gone with the Wind* by pulling out a movie poster from beneath his mattress one time that he'd stolen from a billboard at the cinema in Beirut and insisting to Ibrahim that his mother Philomena— pointing to her picture—looked exactly like Scarlett O'Hara. He could barely pronounce her name and couldn't see the difference between his mother's stern looks and the eyes of the dreamy Hollywood actress.

Jibrail arose from his sick bed and the secret remained suspended between him and his oldest son. They would look at each other and the father would nod his head and the son wouldn't know what he was saying or what he was thinking. Before his death, Jibrail received several visits from his cousin who was affiliated with Internal Security and had certificates and papers no one had seen. The day two months later that the funeral procession for Jibrail went through the streets of the town, children were standing on rooftops to get a good view of the procession. They saw him smiling in the picture the man at the front of the procession was holding. They remembered the pajama pants, his daughter's shrieks, and the taste of the iced *jallab* drink.

From time to time, of her own accord, when Raheel would see her brother Younis—whom she loved, leaving his room in the morning after a heavy sleep, she would tug at his sleeve and keep pointing to the floor of the house, but he wouldn't understand what she meant. He would pat her head affectionately, and before heading toward the door to take the Corvette to Beirut and come back drunk sometimes at a late hour of the night, she'd let out screams from all about the house. All he understood was the word she kept repeating, "English, English" referring to the gold pounds, she who was in the habit of letting out screams for no apparent reason.

5

Younis immediately demanded his father's money, but his brother Ibrahim denied having any cash in his possession. They inquired at the bank, and the manager recalled that their father Jibrail Mubarak had come to his office a year earlier worried that the Lebanese banks were on the brink of insolvency. The manager told him that throughout his past thirty years on the job, clients had been coming to him on a daily basis asking this same question and nothing of the sort ever happened. But Jibrail insisted on closing his account. Their mother brought out the shoebox that her husband had entrusted her with where she kept all the promissory notes that hadn't yet come due.

And so, Ibrahim and Younis entered into a world that their father had always tried to conceal from them. They waited for the first payments to come due, but the only person who showed up was a town schoolteacher who came to pay what he owed on the first of the month, only to come back in the middle of the month to take out a new loan. And another man who said he was the owner of a bicycle shop in the Beirut suburbs came to ask for an extension. He looked desperate, so Ibrahim felt sorry for him and agreed. But before his next payment came due, the bicycle merchant took matters into his own hands. He sold all his bicycles at half-price in a single day and fled the country to evade the money lenders. The other borrowers disregarded the due dates when they heard Jibrail died. So the two brothers divided up the promissory notes, but after Ibrahim made two failed attempts to collect the money owed to his father: one an employee in the Personal Status Department who'd become bedridden with illness and whose salary didn't cover the cost of his medications, as his wife bewailed; the other a widow who wore excessive make-up and continued to gamble rather than pay off her loans. She demanded more money as she hysterically screamed, "Sue me. Put me in jail. Maybe I'll learn my lesson!"—after all that, Ibrahim gave all his promissory notes to Younis. "Congratulations, brother. I don't think I'll be able to call in a single lira from any of these!"

Ibrahim's father had been stingy with him, but he did send him to the American University, to the agricultural branch, which had opened recently. At the university he took classes on soil and plants, and in the coffeeshops he plunged into heated discussions about the role of Islam and Arabic—"the language of the letter _Ḍād_"—in defining Arabism. And when he chose to write about a literary topic for his senior research thesis, he met a smart and shy young woman during the break. They would go for long strolls through the campus gardens, brought together by their shared love of Arabic poetry. Ibrahim tried his best to appease her unsettled emotions and present to her a reassuring picture of what he had in mind for them, and so she clung to him until eventually they got married.

Younis managed to collect on only a few of his father's unpaid loans and blew it all instantly. There was a deep-rooted hostility between him and money, and his expenses increased after he got married and moved to Beirut to get away from his parents and family. He could no longer afford private school tuition, so his children transferred to public school, and he didn't have the money to fix the old Chevy whose motor refused to turn over, so he left it parked outside collecting dust as the air leaked out of the tires. When he ran out of options, he remembered his old accounts. He went to the Land Registry office to obtain a document of title for the family house and Mahmoudiya Orchard, as a first step toward suing to collect his father's inheritance and put his share up for sale.

He was stunned to discover that full ownership of both properties was registered solely in the name of his brother Ibrahim Mubarak. All twenty-four hundred shares. Not his mother, not his sister, and not him. He flew off to Tel Safra fuming with rage. Younis's mother told him that his father had feared he would sell off his inheritance the moment he needed money. What even his mother didn't know was that Jibrail had consulted an expert to estimate the value of the house and the orchard, and then he gave Younis during his life an amount of money equivalent to his share of the inheritance. That explained why he paid out so much money for him the day he'd bought the Corvette and why he gave him double other amounts he'd barely asked for. However, money loses value and real estate gains value. And what Younis could not be compensated for with money was his feeling that they had disowned him, expelled him like some foundling that had been left at their door. He threatened his mother and Ibrahim with cruel punishment he didn't specify and wandered about angrily in a state of disbelief, not knowing where to begin to reclaim what was rightfully his.

In the beginning, the lawyer assured Younis that Lebanese law prohibited a father from excluding any of his sons and did not permit him to disburse more than half of the inheritance by means of a will. In the event that he commenced false sales transactions to a third party who would sell the shares back to the favorite son, it would be easy to raise a case against him for evading this law and thus make the attempt null and void. Afterward, the lawyer obtained a copy of the title that was stamped with the date of ownership and went back to Younis, disappointed and surprised in his turn to tell him that he had fallen victim to a rare loophole concerning transfer of ownership, which he should lecture about at the law school!

When his grandmother Philomena bought the piece of land on which the house was built and the orchard that measured twenty thousand square meters, she proceeded to secretly register it, back in the 1920s, in the name of someone who was not her son, but a man named Asaad al-Saliby, whose mother was Katarina. It was plausible that she had done so because she didn't want to have property in her name in case she became embroiled in a dispute that might arise, leading to seizure of her properties. Younis told the lawyer that the person named on the deed was his father's maternal cousin, and his grandmother must have instructed him to regain possession of the properties for her son Jibrail, who then asked him to register it in the name of his son Ibrahim, since only two names appeared on the real estate documents: Asaad al-Saliby and Ibrahim Mubarak. That historic conspiracy had put an end to the matter. As a result, it was not possible to consider the two properties to be inheritance from Jibrail Mubarak, and there was no way to contest it or make a legal claim since judges ruled based on legal documents not emotions or family narratives.

Younis returned to the town, this time with a moving truck and two movers who followed him through the house. First, he headed directly to Philomena's picture, climbed onto a chair, and took it down from the wall. He held it between his hands and started cursing at her. He placed all the blame on her and called her "Satan in women's clothing." He accused her of having voyaged to America in order to work as a prostitute there and came back solely to sow division in the family. She held the New Testament to feign piety, but the money she'd brought back with her and used to build the house and buy the orchard was sin money that never had, and never would, bear fruit for anyone to enjoy. Then he threw the picture onto the floor, shattering the glass and breaking the frame.

He also brought the clock down from the wall and took it with him, and he grabbed the gramophone that had been placed decoratively in the corner. Most likely he would sell it to an antiques dealer. Then he started dividing up the chairs and the sofas and took everything that was in his bedroom. He even forced his sister Raheel off the couch she was lying on so he could take it, not caring a bit about her screams of protest.

Off he went with a full load.

"You only have relatives on your mother's side," he would repeat afterward to his children. "No relatives on the Mubarak side. You have the right to something that you were denied."

Addressing his two sons he would add, "If you're man enough, you'll go reclaim it."

His mother died and he didn't go to the funeral. His brother Ibrahim got sent to Raml Prison in the capital, and he didn't visit him or even ask about the circumstances surrounding his arrest. His wound was deep and final.

Younis was blessed with three daughters and two sons who

got involved subsequently in the wars that broke out in the capital. Their father so happened to choose a residence for the family in the very neighborhood that sparked the armed civil strife. It was also said that the two sons were involved in the looting of the port's shipping containers and several shopping centers. Their mother was proud of them and loved to show her relatives pictures of them standing behind barricades aiming their weapons. It was as though she and her sister-in-law came from two different planets. Her name was Saideh. She had a loud voice. She'd come to the capital from a mountain village way up north, the daughter of a family of farmers. She delivered babies while walking down the street. She'd breastfeed them for a long time and then set them loose.

Whereas her sister-in-law Emily felt it to be an unparalleled event to bring a child into the world and then see him grow up. She gave birth to Zakariya and thought she was finished with that ordeal, but Ibrahim persuaded her to do it again. Then she begged for them to stop. Her heart would break at the mere sight of pictures of her children when they were little, standing next to the water spring or on Palm Sunday in their new white outfits. Emily spent a lot of time by herself at the window in her bedroom—hers and Ibrahim's—that overlooked the valley. She would read and sometimes she would write in her diary, in Arabic at times and in English at others. She never went to church even on Sundays, and there was nothing about her behavior that suggested faith of any sort. She waited a long time before baptizing Zakariya. Her desire, which she didn't dare make known—to let him choose his religion for himself when he came of age—didn't last for long before her in-laws.

Emily came from a family who, with the arrival of American missionaries to Lebanon, switched from the Orthodox faith to the incoming Protestant denomination. Her religious education was broadened, while her faith cooled to lukewarm. Over the course of two centuries, the family had dispersed between Jerusalem, Damascus, and Beirut. Emily had relatives in all three cities. Her horizons widened and she came to have numerous questions about the meaning of life. She'd found in Ibrahim a young man with an easy-going nature, a good listener; his voice was soft and warm. So, she agreed to follow him to his hometown. She loved him and he loved her, and they never argued a single day. She shared the burden of taking care of Raheel with her mother-in-law. Emily had the face of a Red Cross worker and an unsettled, tormented inner self that she only revealed in the pages of her diary.

She went to live with him at his family's home, hoping to help them get back together. She encouraged her son Zakariya to pay an unannounced visit to his uncle Younis. Things did not improve, but a truce in the war between the brothers was struck up after Younis came home to his house in Beirut that evening, whistling and waving a big check in front of his face, his commission for acting as a middleman in the sale of an old building on behalf of a real estate company that planned to build a skyscraper on top of it. Then, as though he would never get used to being financially secure, it didn't last long, for Younis died from a surgical error, which only increased his family's feelings of being persecuted.

The fighting near the house quieted down only to have a new, deadlier war break out when Israeli tanks rolled in near Tel Safra, whose inhabitants had managed to stay out of the fighting, thanks to a mutual understanding among its people. Four from the town were killed and a few others were injured in a sudden bombardment no one was expecting, and which people said was the result of an error in the cannon's coordinates. That gratuitous massacre had just one positive aspect—the random bombs brought down two casualties from among the Druze and two from among the Christians, which prevented any friction between the two sides. In fact, the town witnessed an exchange of condolences and shared participation in the memorial ceremonies. One of the bombs strayed in the direction of the Mubarak home, burning a walnut tree, and making a hole in the red roof tiles. The windows were all shattered, and Philomena's picture fell onto the floor again. Ibrahim had fixed it before renovating the ceiling and had put it back up on the wall, having remembered what his father told him the day he had his commemorative photo taken.

He had forgotten all about it because he had put his grandmother's secret in the same category as the rumors that were passed from generation to generation about the existence of buried treasures in the town in the vicinity of the Roman Temple of Astarte. There was always someone out digging at night, trying to find the treasure of Eshmoun Azar or the jewels of Queen Elissar without finding anything to quench their thirst. Over his cherished after-lunch cup of coffee, he told the story like some entertaining fairy tale to his wife and Zakariya and Marta and sick Raheel who was hearing about that treasure for the second time.

That evening, Emily wrote the following in her diary.

All sorts of tales about the Mubarak family have been woven around my husband's grandmother Philomena. They say that she knew the time of her death to the exact hour and that she told her son just one day before-hand about a treasure buried beneath the house—this beautiful house that we inherited from her where I am writing now beside one of the windows. As for my hus-band's father Jibrail—and I'm not sure who decided to choose all the family names from the Holy Bible—he made a bit of a mistake in his hour of death and relayed the "secret" of the buried gold to his eldest son two months before he died. Ibrahim told us that same story today, which doesn't set my mind at ease even though my husband is in good health, "to entertain us," as he said. It reminded me of a story I read about a man who went searching for a treasure he'd seen in a dream. He roamed the whole world, only to come back to find it right near his own house. Philomena had tasted the bitterness of immigration. She sailed the seas all by herself. So, she invented this fib so that her son and his descendants would cling to their birthplace, so they wouldn't dare sell the house. She interpreted Jesus' statement, "For where your treasure is, there your heart will be also," as she liked, literally. She was shrewder than that, too, when she added the notion that digging up the gold in the cellar would put the whole house at risk of collapsing. That way the illusion would remain an illusion, never being discovered and never dying.

And Emily added to her diary after pausing from writing for more than a week:

I wept from the depths of my being. All my fears came true. The world has slammed shut on me and Zakariya and Marta. After he told us about his grandmother's gold, the very next day, another bomb hit us from the same cannon position that had fired missiles at the

town "by mistake," as they'd claimed. A missile coming
to the same target as though it had been late arriving
with the others. It shook the house with us inside,
killing Ibrahim instantly. He was watering the roses
at the front steps.

With his father now dead and the capital having transformed into a bloody theater even during interruptions in operations, Zakariya decided to leave the country. His mother no longer had anything in her bag of tricks to convince him to stay. She told him that she and her brother divided the family inheritance amicably and that she decided to give her eldest son the largest share of her cash money in dollars. And so, he left behind his mother, his sister, and his aunt, who Marta accused of having told Younis's sons—whom she called "the orphans"—about the gold. She caught her one time holding the phone and repeating her usual phrase in a loud voice, "English gold, English gold." But Emily said she was just imitating the way the family talked into the phone and had no idea how to use it.

The truth was that it was Marta who made the story known and not her aunt. Once there were no men left in the house, she couldn't bear the idea of constantly having her hands tied, so she brought a Bedouin from the Beqaa valley—an expert at excavating wells and digging up treasures, who swore to her there was water or "metal" under the house. He showed her how the pomegranate branch "quivered" in the vicinity of the second column that carried the weight of the arches. He told her he was prepared to excavate there in return for a quarter of whatever he found. But she, too, decided to postpone her decision.

After the Bedouin's visit to the Mubaraks', news spread that there were fifty kilograms of gold under the house. It was unknown how they came up with the figure fifty kilograms, but the news reached Younis's sons like salt landing on a wound. They sent a letter in the mail demanding their share of the house and the orchard; Philomena was their great-grandmother, and no one was allowed to deprive them of their rightful inheritance. Marta answered them in writing saying, "Your father ate up his share during his lifetime," and in any case she didn't own any of it, not her and not her mother. Zakariya had left the country, and she had no idea where on earth he'd landed. They persisted for years, alternating between making demands and threats and placing all blame on their cousin and claiming they couldn't just be cut off like a branch from a tree. During that summer when Zakariya returned, they tried calling him repeatedly on his cell phone, and when he decided one time to pick up and heard his cousin demanding to have the gold pounds that were buried beneath the house, Zakariya told him they should "have some sense" because the whole thing was nothing but a fairytale. His cousin on the other end of the phone immediately responded that Zakariya was just lying to keep them away from the treasure. Zakariya looked at his great-grandmother's picture with rebuke for having pushed that story. He felt as though she was looking back at him harshly as if to blame him because this time, he had revealed her true secret…

6

News of Zakariya's murder spread all over town, and along with it—simultaneously and in whispers—came the names of his two cousins. For every victim in those parts, there was always an enemy who has declared his animosity openly, a well-known enemy with well-known motives.

There was talk of a man in the 1930s who'd shot his enemy and went to the authorities to turn himself in. But the French officer insisted on getting statements from some women who had witnessed the incident to prove the murder attempt. He took the women to the jail where they refused to reveal the name of their relative who had committed the crime. The man, in turn, requested a meeting with the women to urge them to confess and go back home to their children. "Is that what you would have wanted, you whores? That someone other than me had shot him?"

The morning after Zakariya's body was found, and before any details from the police station or the hospital were released, the card players at the coffeehouse kept bringing up the name Gibran—Younis Mubarak's "little" son. They were well aware of the cruel nature he'd inherited from his mother's side of the family. For them, that was all there was to it. Case closed, court adjourned, back to business as usual.

And as is usually the case when the deceased is a young man or the victim of murder, the president and members of the Municipal Council attended the funeral with sullen faces, along with nuns from the Two Holy Hearts School, who offered their condolences in French, and Druze clerics in their baggy black *sirwal* pants and white skullcaps, who whispered among themselves placing the blame on parents who don't treat their children equally. Even the parish priest was overcome with zeal during his sermon at the funeral, rebuking relatives who turn to their guns to solve their financial disputes and finishing up with a rundown of Zakariya's fine qualities—a man he'd met only once but had found to be of good character and strong faith—and a prayer for compassion to fill people's hearts, one and all.

Meanwhile, in addition to the preliminary report and the medical examiner's report, the Office of the Prosecutor in Beirut received a phone call at around noon from the sergeant at the town police station, saying the victim's sister was also making loud accusations against her cousins living in Beirut. The sergeant was nervous and rushing to close the case after having sent everything he had found on the victim to the prosecutor, with the exception of the Glock 17, which would now put him under suspicion and make him subject to penalty, even if he were to change his mind and decide to report the gun later on. The detectives began checking the addresses of Younis Mubarak's sons in the Ain el-Remmaneh neighborhood as a first step toward bringing them in to serve as witnesses in the case. The townspeople up in the mountain slept peacefully at night with the feeling that the case would soon be solved and that such a heinous crime could never happen to them, because all of them had succeeded in divvying up their parents' inheritance with their brothers and sisters without excluding or upsetting anyone.

The surprise came to them the next day. At eleven o'clock in the morning, the sexton entered the congregation hall, looking behind himself as if he had some news to share, but he was unable to because Younis Mubarak's sons suddenly appeared at the door. They were wearing black neckties. The youngest came forward first with his sure steps and stiff expression, followed by his hesitant older brother with that permanent smile on his face. They embraced Marta who became flustered, her complexion turning even paler and her eyes becoming frozen with anger.

They sat down and softly apologized for missing the funeral. The news hadn't reached them until only hours before, and by mere coincidence. Marta couldn't find anything to say in response. Several times she thought about heading home but she stayed, and everyone stayed. They sat in tense silence in front of curious onlookers from the town who'd come back to the hall to see with their own eyes what those who had taken their turn the day before had seen. They didn't want to miss out on any interesting developments which were not long in coming. Upon exiting unaccompanied, the two brothers found the young lieutenant and the group of soldiers who had been hastily called in to Tel Safra following the discovery of the crime waiting for them at the entrance, along with the sergeant.

Younis Mubarak's sons reiterated the facts of their dispute with their cousins over ownership of the orchard and the house, swearing that neither of them had stepped foot in the town for years on account of their falling out. But that didn't mean they denied their blood relation or dared to be arrogant in the face of death. The sergeant feared the situation might become complicated if they proved their innocence, for he too had slept easy the night before over a crime with a known perpetrator, so he claimed a witness had seen them speeding away in a car at sundown two days earlier. They scoffed at him and vehemently denied the accusation. The lieutenant believed them, eyeing the sergeant with reproach as he gave them an official summons to come to the Government Palace in Baabda.

There, the two men were brought before Kamal Abu Khalid, the assistant investigating judge for the Mount Lebanon region. They presented to Abu Khalid the names of acquaintances who could attest to their presence in Beirut at the time the crime was committed. One of them, Gibran, had been at a seaside coffee shop smoking a *nargileh* with some friends. The other, the eldest, had been at Saint Rita's Church attending Sunday Mass. They both denied having murdered Zakariya and high-lighted once again how they had been left out of the Mubarak family inheritance. So, the young detective advised them to raise a legal case to reclaim their rights, not having been told that they already tried that and failed. He released them on lack of evidence but also cautioned them it might become necessary to request further documentation as the case developed.

Now that the certainty that relatives were to blame had un-raveled, conjecturing veered in every possible direction this time. Some continued to cling to the cousins as suspects, though, believing what they'd seen with their own eyes—even if only once in their lives—how people sometimes killed someone and then marched at his funeral.

The bereaved Marta showed the detective a couple of threatening letters she'd received from her cousins. He glanced over them briefly after noticing the postmark going back more than ten years. He asked for more, so she told him about the phone calls and text messages in recent years, which she would erase every time because she got so angry and anxious whenever she received them and read them. "It was like getting an electric shock."

When he asked her about her brother, her eyes welled up with tears. She pulled out a wad of tissues from her purse and began haphazardly narrating to him the biography of a gentle, cultured man who couldn't hurt a soul, who loved trees and cultivating them, an expert like his father on grapes and wine. He went abroad and had his fill of women and traveling. She was going to live alone now in that house, she and her aunt Raheel. She was sure she would lose her mind in the near future, just like her aunt. She didn't sleep a wink the two nights following his death.

He'd been sad during his last days. From the kitchen, she could hear him sighing heavily while lying down in the living room, looking up at the colorful etchings in the gypsum on the ceiling. Sometimes he would smile at the picture of his great-grandmother Philomena. He had been staying in his parents' bedroom. He'd lock the door with the key whenever he left the house, and he was always there in the room whenever she came to tidy up. She saw him once holding a dark glass bottle and kissing it with his eyes closed. She wasn't able to get inside the room now because the key had been in his pocket and the policeman took it. The judge advised her against opening the door by force. She concluded by saying that when she told Zakariya what their mother had said before she died, that the best thing to ever happen to her was to die before her two children, he locked himself in the room. And he wouldn't come out until she threatened to call the neighbors for help. She didn't think there was anyone besides their cousins who wanted to hurt him, but he was above all that. She heard him saying one time that he wanted to sell the orchard and was thinking about giving half the proceeds to his cousins. He wanted to be done with the owners of the land surrounding the orchard. They were tiresome and were going to cause him a lot of grief. They hadn't forgotten about the incident with his father. Here she started crying again, for herself this time, because in the end Zakariya had become her father and her mother…

The detective didn't interrupt her. He surrendered himself to the story of Zakariya Mubarak, but Marta was a machine that never stopped and was not of any use because she went off in every direction. She eventually got tired, so he saw her to the door and went back to his office to phone the town police station. He warned the sergeant about the consequences of making offhanded statements, reminding him that his report did not document the exact hour and minute. And also, he hadn't found the cartridge that had undoubtedly fallen from the revolver or rifle. He told him to go back to the crime scene and look for it. He also hadn't summoned the forensics team to come take fingerprints. He warned him not to try to get ahead of the investigation or influence it with summonses and accusations. The sergeant hung up the phone and fired off a couple of crude curses.

Kamal Abu Khalid read the medical examiner's report and found it pretty bland. He pushed it aside and sent the enclosed bullet to the ballistics lab. He picked up the belongings that were found on Zakariya at the time of the murder and took with his other hand for a picture of Zakariya so he could have a mental image of him to keep in mind. He found one of him standing in a public park in front of a stone statue of the god Eros shooting his arrow toward the sky; most likely it was in Paris. He found another one of him with a woman at Caffè Florian, both daydreaming, each one looking off in a different direction, in San Marcos square in Venice. He paused on a picture of him holding up a little girl and gobbling her up with his eyes beneath an almond tree full of white blossoms. Wherever he was, it was spring. That was the girl in the picture Zakariya had sewn into his undershirt, which his sister Marta had handed over to him, covered in blood, saying she didn't know who the girl was. The detective found himself eagerly spying on this man who'd been surrounded by women, plucking out the details of his life.

He finished looking through the pictures, and before downloading everything from the cell phone, he turned his attention to the papers that had been found in Zakariya's pockets: a certificate from Marc Chagall that had a stamp from the artist's studio and Chagall's signature clearly showing his first and last name, written with utmost care rather than signed, dated 5/7/1981, a certificate in which the artist attests that the painting "The Blue Violinist" was painted with oil on a 40 x 70 cm linen canvas; a typed list of all the varieties of grape plants in the various regions of France and the best type of soil for Merlot or Riesling grapes or Chardonnay; a letter written in English signed by "Mary" telling her father what she had done over the course of a day in her little life. She'd sat in the back seat on the school bus where she liked to sit every day so she could keep waving to him with both arms until the bus turned the corner and he went out of view. She liked Carole more than all her other classmates and she loved him most of all out of everyone. She was going to be a bird with two wings in the school play on the last day before summer break.

The lives of the murder victims Kamal Abu Khalid had investigated over the past three years while in his post had been simple and straightforward. They hadn't demanded much from him. There was no mystery to obscure their situations: drug smuggling, burglary attempts, kidnappings motivated by money, and sometimes honor killings such as the murder of a wife accused of adultery, or suicides resulting from cases of schizophrenia that had increased in recent years. Zakariya Mubarak's circumstances appeared to be more complicated, and the magistrate was happy for the challenge. He went back to the pictures on the victim's cell phone, looking at Zakariya standing in the doorway of White Elephant Restaurant, reassuring him, "Don't worry. They're not going to get away with what they did!"

When he returned to looking at the text messages, he found what one might expect: an apology in French for being late for a meeting and best wishes for safe travels; condolences in English for the death of his mother Emily, "I know how close you were to her and how difficult it is for you to lose her while being so far away. You cannot leave Mary all alone. All my love. You are courageous." Mary was most likely his daughter.

Then he found some crass questions like, "You left a lot of clothes here that belong to you. What would you like me to do with them?" or grieved ones from women like, "You made a hole in my heart that is so hard to fill."

There were a large number of messages, and Kamal was not prepared to hand them over to any of his assistants. He didn't trust their intelligence or precision. He pored over them in succession until he arrived at one that said, "In regard to our agreement in the City of Lights, I've learned that there are numerous musicians on the market and in various guises attributed to the same composer." He paused at this sentence that had been crafted so as to cause confusion; it was the kind of wording that concealed other meanings. He went on to read the next message which had been sent from the same international number as the message that talked about musicians. "Our friend will visit you soon in your hometown to hand you the gift and to settle once and for all the matter of the violinist. Watch over it carefully."

Kamal Abu Khalid quickly pieced the picture together. Zakariya Mubarak had come back from his travels abroad with Chagall's valuable painting, which was up for sale, in his possession. He forbade even his sister from entering his room because that's where he'd hidden the painting. And, judging by the measurements mentioned on the artist's certificate, it must be worth a lot of money if it was an original as it appeared to be. There might be more than one dead body to come out of a deal like that…

His enthusiasm grew stronger, and he started feeling convinced that he had discovered some semblance of a motive for the crime. He'd read all the messages without adding any more items to his list of clues. The next day, he slipped Zakariya's key into his pocket and headed for the town without calling Marta to tell her he was coming. He broke the acknowledged protocol, which assumed that he would hand over the items to the Judiciary Police to finish their investigation before submitting a report to him with the results. But his evaluation of the considerable financial stake behind what he had discovered after researching the exorbitant prices for Chagall's paintings, which apparently had even surprised the artist himself while he was alive, and his fear of the widespread tampering of evidence among law enforcement, made him decide to finish the investigation himself. He took off in his car the next morning.

Marta opened the door for him. The picture of the woman with a book in her hand appeared to him from the entrance. He asked Marta who she was, to which she answered with a dejected sigh, "My great-grandmother Philomena…"

Pointing to the old woman stretched out on the sofa, she said, "…and that's my aunt Raheel. Ever since my brother went abroad, she's been asking for him, and now she might not understand that he's dead."

"When did your brother go abroad?"

"Right after the Israelis withdrew from Beirut, the moment the airport reopened."

7

Zakariya Mubarak boarded the plane the same day Halley's comet flashed across the sky. At home, the morning of his departure, his aunt Raheel sat on one of his suitcases speaking deliriously in her half-words, repeating the names of her mother and her grandmother Philomena in a hopeless attempt to stop him from leaving.

His mother walked him to the door and held him by the shoulders, letting his face be stamped in her memory. She closed her eyes and hugged him for a long time and then turned around and went to her room. When evening fell, the time when Emily warded off her melancholy by writing, she discovered that Zakariya had stolen her diary. She shrugged her shoulders and smiled tenderly. She saw his face again and knew deep in her heart that after today she would never see him again.

Crying at Beirut airport was still common then, and Zakariya's sister Marta did just that while saying her goodbyes. Some Muslim pilgrims on their way to the Hajj, whose flight to

Saudi Arabia had been delayed, saw how she sobbed while sitting there in the waiting area and then pulled out an embroidered handkerchief and loudly blew her nose into it. When they called for his flight to begin boarding, Zakariya hugged her close to him and then pulled her aside and whispered something in her ear that caused her to let out a loud scream as if she was having a heart attack. On the way back along the winding road to the town, the driver giving her a ride heard her talking to herself. "He'll come back, he'll come back. I stole his watch and hid it from him…"

Zakariya sat on the plane next to a Frenchman with smiling eyes, red cheeks, and breath that smelled of red wine. He revealed to Zakariya as they flew over the Turkish city of Galatasaray that he was bisexual and "went out" with a guy or a gal, no difference. To get away from him, Zakariya got up and walked to the bathroom, and when he came back the man was snoring, the sports magazine *L'Équipe* covering his face.

Zakariya brought the cash with him that he'd gotten from his mother. He had tucked the better part of it inside the lining of his jacket, as his mother had advised, and hopped off the plane looking handsome, with a spring in his step. He liked the cold sting of the Paris air and bought a scarf from a sidewalk vendor who told him it was pure cashmere. He carefully tied it around his neck after checking how other pedestrians were wearing theirs. He took notice of the colors of the men's suit jackets and the style of their trousers. Two weeks after moving in near Place de la Bastille, Zakariya Mubarak—aided by his diaphanous white complexion and his eye color that teetered between blue and green—looked like a French history teacher who belonged to the Socialist Party and was committed to environmental issues. The Mubarak family tendency toward early balding left its mark on

Zakariya, so he covered it up with a French worker cap for a few days before switching for good—right up until the day he was killed—to a black cowboy hat in winter and a straw Panama hat, real or imitation, with its red band in summer.

He quit gazing at the statues of philosophers and writers erected in the parks and squares, and reading the headlines in the morning newspapers, and with time he started walking along like the city locals, looking neither left nor right, as if he was in a hurry to get to his destination, though he had no idea where he was going. He likewise became skilled at looking straight ahead and not turning his head whenever the sidewalk became crowded with beautiful women. He stopped only to watch the fat accordionist with the depressing face and peppy music. He would drop some coins into his hat and then turn into the nearby café to reminisce about his parents' house on the mountainside, drenched in sunlight. Raheel holds her head in her hands and stumbles over her words, Emily breaks in a new diary, pouring her heart into it while trying to stifle coughing fits that overpower her and for which she refuses to go see the doctor. Marta, with her difficult taste in men, makes detailed and careful plans for her potential marriage. Even after being informed of his mother's passing, he continued to imagine the three of them there. Three women with only one male family member left—himself.

The city draws him back in. At a dimly lit bar he orders an "Irish coffee," not knowing what it tastes like but liking its name. He reads on the metro, seated beside a woman noisily scolding herself in Spanish. He flips through the pages of *Muluk al-Arab* (Kings of the Arabs), one of ten books his mother had carefully selected for him and packed in his bags so he wouldn't forget his mother tongue. He read even while standing in line, at the courtyard of the Grand Ballet where a retrospective exhibit of Edward Hopper was being held, and there, while inching forward one step at a time, he sensed that the woman in line behind him was peeking over his shoulder.

He turned around and smiled at her. She smiled back and asked if that was Hebrew he was reading. He said his name was Zakariya, but he didn't know any Hebrew. He closed Ameen Rihani's book and opened up to the woman who was his same height and spoke intermittently about the beautiful weather that was convenient during their wait in line, and the bus driver strike that was making life in the city difficult.

After a while, he turned all the way around to face her. She moved forward as he moved backward, which made them laugh, and laughing opens the heart for more. Her beauty was perfect, at its peak. She'd come close to the moment of equilibrium between the cheerful and hesitant days of youth and an advancement in age when a slump would not be long in coming, like a piece of ripe fruit that should not be left too long to whither. She held his hands and guided him to prevent him from bumping into the person ahead of him or to speed him up. They brushed against each other, got to know each other, and turned the boredom of waiting in line into something enjoyable that neither of them wanted to end.

Inside the various rooms of the exhibit, they didn't talk about the paintings by "the artist of loneliness, cityscapes, and the call of the unknown." They talked about themselves.

About him—Zakariya—that he didn't really know Hopper but had heard of him from an artist friend of his in Beirut who secretly imitated his work. But he was noticing now that the subjects of his friend's paintings were happier.

About her, that she would be leaving at the end of the day

on a night train to the south. She loved night trains with their whistles blowing as she passed through little cities, sound asleep.

About him, that soon he would be taking a class on grape growing and wine making because Noah—the original wine-grower—had lived in Zakariya's hometown or a short distance from it, and that he had an orchard there that was drenched in sunshine and was waiting for his return.

About her, that she owned a hotel in a small city "over there—across from your country."

About him, that his mother didn't want him to get married. She was afraid of children, of their life, and of their death.

About her, that she was recently divorced and had a son named Jean-Baptiste. She spoke the name and then noticed the coincidence. They looked at each other in silent shock: Zechariah and John the Baptist!

They burst out laughing and nearly embraced each other.

About him, that he wasn't attracted to women from his homeland. They made him feel incestuous.

They each chose details and tidbits from their lives to share to entice the other and make the other feel he or she could delve deeper unobstructed. But that did not happen. The potential for sharing feelings for each other got postponed. They left the exhibit, walked down the sidewalk together a few meters, shook hands warmly. She gave him her business card saying, "If you happen to pass that way, maybe I will need a man to help me run the hotel."

Mathilde Lagrange
Sunflower Hotel
Fédéric Mistral Square
Saint-Paul-de-Vence

He had been surrounded by women at home and at the College of Business Administration in Beirut. His female classmates trusted him with their secrets. He fixed the problems they had with their boyfriends. They lent him money if his pockets were empty. They sat in his lap. Jealousy had no place in his heart; he was unemotional toward those tender-hearted virgins, whereas a mature woman like Mathilde enchanted him with her beauty, her divorce, her motherhood, and the fact she was older than him. He found himself tucking her card in between the pages of his passport where it was sure not to get lost.

He wandered with no clear desires. Then he worked as a manager at a restaurant called *Le Cèdre du Liban*—the Cedar of Lebanon. The owner, who chain-smoked American cigarettes, gave him an interview, subjecting him to an interrogation in which he did not ask about his experience managing restaurants or with Lebanese cuisine, but rather wanted to know first what his name was, what his father's name was, and all the way to his grandfather Jibrail. From this he could be certain he was Christian. Then they struck up a peculiarly Lebanese conversation.

"What family are you from?"

"The Mubarak family."

"I know some Mubaraks from east Sidon."

"We're from Tel Safra, up over Beirut. They say our ancestors came from north Lebanon."

"All the Mubaraks I know are Roman Catholic."

"We're Maronites."

A wide grin took shape on the man's face. He apologized to his interlocutor and said that actually he had employees working for him "from all denominations," as he said, but only trusted Maronites. Zakariya learned later on that he was called "the Albino" because of his blond hair and freckled face. He'd gained notoriety during the civil war. He had an intimidating demeanor and was surrounded by assistants of his from the fighting who had moved with him into the Lebanese restaurant business abroad. Zakariya took the job, which seemed below his qualifications after realizing that the wad of money from his mother in his leather jacket was getting thinner by the day and wouldn't last more than six months.

His work shift was difficult. He was only allowed one day off per week. He supervised the workers, organized wedding banquets and family dinners for Lebanese expatriates who liked to dine together in large groups. He took the checks and cash to the bank, mingled with customers. A woman always dressed in sky blue or derivative colors would come sometimes at noon. She asked him about what was going on in his homeland and was pleased with his explanation of the ingredients for Aleppo kibbeh with pomegranate and mushrooms and his concluding remark that globalization made its first appearances on the dinner table. She liked his cleverness and erudition, and invited him to "Tuesday Sessions" at her home where she brought him together with a few admirers of her writing. She'd published seven books and was working on the eighth. As in all the preceding books, she revived the specter of a stern father who'd retired from military service in Algeria and imposed his power with his silence. A tender mother who spent her day sighing, who liked to crochet and befriend flowers and cats. A disturbed brother dressed in black who eventually ended up in a hospital for mental illness where she visits him once a month. She delivered all that in poetry at times and in short stories at other times. Her guests, who were not stingy about praising her fine sentiments, would clap for her, and she said she was a good cook, enjoyed writing, and the only thing she was missing was the love she'd lost long ago. She said this while gazing into Zakariya's eyes. He had become one of the mainstays of the group whose sessions now were only scheduled on his day off. Then attendance at the sessions started to dwindle, until it was reduced to no one but the owner of the house and Zakariya, tête-à-tête, and she bribed him by telling him she was going to write a diwan of poetry about him called, "The Man Who Came from the East." He spent two months in the cage of love. He got bored with spending hours in bed and listening to poetic images. Then one clear day, he took off without warning. So, she modified the title of her new short story collection to "The Woman Who Doesn't Know How to Hold on to Her Man."

The owner of *Le Cèdre du Liban* sent him to Africa where he had opened a restaurant in Dakar and another in Yaoundé. Zakariya checked in on the kitchen, helped with food preparation and menu enhancement. He was first to serve tabbouleh without bulghur wheat to customers from Arab communities, and even the local black bourgeoisie, and also introduced adding cherries to *kefta* with pine nuts and pomegranate paste. He would inaugurate a new restaurant with a spectacular evening celebration and make sure it got off to a solid start before moving on to London and then to Moscow to open another location, and no matter where he went, food was the key to women's hearts.

He went through some strange phases, like when he persevered three months in an intimate relationship with a Polish woman whose name he forgot because it was too difficult to pronounce and write down the day he decided to make a list of women he'd taken to bed. He didn't know a single word of her language. She squealed with delight whenever she tasted the ice cream with cotton candy or *halawet el-rizz*—rice and cheese cream—that he made for her himself, exactly the way she squealed when making love, and then started crying immediately afterward. She'd scream strange proper nouns before singing a lullaby to herself that she remembered from her mother, and then Zakariya would hold her and she would fall asleep, exhausted, in his arms.

By coincidence, or perhaps by a subconscious tendency on his part, he always seemed to land in the path of older women, until one time he got entangled in a romantic relationship with a mother and daughter. He would go back and forth between their apartments, like in some low-budget movie, cover up his meetings with them, lie, and cook for both of them until he got fed up with it all as usual and left after stealing from each of them a small memento: a brassiere or a hairpin. He'd disappear, leaving behind emotions that had not yet withered and clothes in the bedroom closet that he couldn't have removed without raising their suspicions. He'd leave his hat behind, to force himself to buy a new one. He'd leave without a note or a phone call. He timed his break-ups when the relationship was at its best because he'd come to realize that in the coming days boredom was guaranteed to spring up and overrun the relationship like weeds.

These adventures continued without side effects until the devil whispered to Zakariya to respond to the attention the wife of his benefactor the Albino was showing him in the form of glances whose meaning was clear. The owner of the *Le Cèdre du Liban* restaurant chain did a lot of traveling, and it became evident later that his investments in Lebanese cuisine were just a front for laundering profits from illegal business dealings he had between Africa and Europe. His choice of specific capital cities to open new restaurants was tied to activities he had in them with associates, some of whom were known to Interpol and others with a foot in organized crime. His Argentinian wife was struck with a severe case of boredom, as might be expected, in her husband's absence. Despite Zakariya's taking all possible precautions to wait until her husband went away and never meet up with her twice at the same hotel, a young, ambitious employee took it upon himself to expose them. He sent an anonymous letter to the boss, who in turn proceeded to interrogate his wife with a leather belt in hand and threatened to send her back to her destitute parents in Argentina, until she broke down in tears, admitted her guilt, and swore to him that she had been the one who seduced Zakariya and made an appeal to him never to leave her alone for long periods of time from that day forward.

The "Albino" didn't show any resentment toward Zakariya and continued to assign him duties here and there. But one night in Moscow, Zakariya was assaulted and suffered a brutal beating at the hands of two gigantic, masked men who beat him while spewing out curses at him in Russian. They dumped him on the sidewalk out in front of the apartment building where he lived. Zakariya believed he'd been the victim of mistaken identity, but then on a trip to Cameroon he was hit with a charge of embezzlement based on fabricated evidence the moment he arrived in Yaoundé. They threatened to put him in jail unless he paid back the money he hadn't actually taken. And that was where his relationship with the Lebanese food business ended, when one of the Cameroon policemen told him, "The Albino says hello."

He paid a lot for the sake of women he was not at all sure he loved, especially the Albino's wife who kept praying to the black Our Lady of Guadalupe the whole time she was cheating on her husband. She would make the sign of the cross whenever taking off in a car or if she rode an elevator to the highest floors. In Yaoundé, they gave him a choice between sending him back to Lebanon or to France, so he chose France because he had opened a secret bank account for himself there when he was making good money and also because he couldn't imagine going back to his mother and sister a broken man. After a few days back in Paris, he called the house several times but hung up the phone as soon as he heard Marta's voice on the other end.

He bought a used Citroën and drove south Saint-Paul-de-Vence.

8

Above the reception desk was a black-and-white photograph of the entrance to the Sunflower Hotel, showing how it had looked back in the middle of the twentieth century. Behind the desk sat a man, in his sixties, who had a slender physique and nervous temperament. Jerome. His name was engraved on a name tag above the lapel of his jacket. He looked suspiciously at Zakariya the moment he entered. He wasn't going to call for Mathilde before getting Zakariya's name and asking with curiosity what it was that he needed her for, when she suddenly came in through the back door. She gasped in surprise before giving Zakariya a warm embrace that he wasn't expecting, and neither was Jerome, who had surrendered to the existence of this relationship he'd known nothing about. Mathilde whispered to Zakariya in a hushed voice while pointing to the group of Japanese tourists gathered in the small lobby, "Don't worry. They're all leaving this afternoon."

She got straight to the point right from the start. They took a good look at each other for a few seconds. He noticed a lack of luster in her eyes and some wrinkles on her neck.

"You look younger," she said, as though she'd read his mind.

They finished the verbal swordplay that they had begun in Paris, as though four years had never elapsed. They picked up where they'd left off, before Mathilde Lagrange took a taxi to Lyon train station, holding her purse over her head to block the first drops of rain.

The first day, they celebrated. They sat in the garden behind the hotel over a chilled bottle of expensive white wine. He propped his chin on the palm of his hand and gazed at her face. She armed herself with silence and then said that she always expected him to come, never gave up on waiting for him. Pulling her card out from his passport he said, "I saved your card as ammunition against hard times."

She smiled, not getting her fill of gazing at him either. He fit her image of an ideal man. He answered her, after a couple swigs of wine, that she had surprised him in Paris. She'd appeared to him from an unexpected place, from Hopper's nighttime cafes, from the mysteriousness of the women there, from places he didn't know and would never come to know.

They stayed that way late into the night, under the illusion that what coincidence had woven for them was rare, until they got tired of digging up their feelings and coining them into eloquent and seductive words. They started interrupting their exchange of words with gentle finger touches and light caresses on the cheek or arm. All the talking had paved the way for the hot French kisses that exploded between them once the hotel activity died down at around midnight, as was heralded by the clock at the Church of Saint-Julien-le-Pauvre in Frédéric Mistral Square. A fiery embrace that should have happened the moment he stepped out of the Citroën and appeared in the hotel doorway with his hat tipped to the side and his red suitcase in tow.

Their bodies stuck together from the first night when he carried her upstairs to the bedroom with the view of the blue horizon, the one on the second floor that she gave him when he first arrived. He stumbled, panting, her arms around his neck as he tried to fish out his key and open the door. They tumbled onto the bed, took off their clothes while lying down, not parting from each other, and stayed up until the first rays of dawn appeared. They revealed to each other later that they would never forget that May night. Mathilde said that the planets had been in rare alignment that day: the moon, Mercury, and Venus were in a perfectly straight line. Zakariya smiled and said he'd been born under the sign of Virgo.

"Virgo?"

Her eyes popped in surprise because her intuition was confirmed—it was the optimal time for their love to spark. He didn't tell her, of course, that he had recently discovered the true date of his birth in his mother's diary. It wasn't the date written on his ID and in astrological terms would place him under the sign of Aquarius.

Over the days that followed, they proceeded to calibrate their emotions and their view of what was happening between them. Mathilde declared she was wary of falling in love. She wanted love to be complete and was afraid it would fall apart. And Zakariya was carried away by the same tune, and mixed, with utmost ease, true feelings with those fake ones he'd come across in some of his readings or in things others said about passionate love. He wasn't the ladies' man that one might imagine, for he didn't lie and would get caught up in feelings at the beginning of things, or at least in expressing those feelings, and then he'd spend the rest of the time trying to free himself of them. To anyone who knew his family and its history, Zakariya was a contradictory combination of his grandfather Jibrail, who nothing could stop from going after women other than his own embarrassment about his unforeseen inability to satisfy them at that time, and his mother Emily, from whom he'd inherited his gentleness and cheerful disposition and who he was now getting to know in her various life stages from the pages of her thick diary.

After they came to an emotional agreement with each other, which is the common pact between lovers at the beginning of the road and which the two had undoubtedly concluded numerous times during their previous romances, Mathilde paraded him all around the hotel. She would exchange kisses on the cheek with some of the male patrons, introduce him to the workers and reception staff on the day and night shifts as their new manager. She went over the price lists with him and the discounts available to travel agencies according to the season.

He was talented. He left a mark wherever he worked and made it difficult to manage without him. He responded person- ally to the customers' calls and complaints. He put his nose in all the details. He longed for the kitchen but couldn't find a way to introduce his favorite dishes to the traditional French menu at the Sunflower. The first of every month he'd find a check signed by Mathilde Lagrange on his desk: a respectable sum on top of his being, as they say, "watered and foddered" like the national cavalry.

She would leave him on his own and go away twice a month without disclosing her destination or the reason for her absence. He was an excellent proxy. The hotel employees all loved him, but his first attempt in gaining the affection of Jean Baptiste, Mathilde's only son, was unsuccessful, until some carefully chosen gifts produced the desired effect. The ice melted and he started joining him on hot days on trips to the beach. Zakariya spent two years at the hotel as if undercover, known only by his first name: Zachary. If any of his own people came into the reception area, he refrained from speaking a word of Arabic and pretended to be busy at a good distance from their curious eyes. But he kept up with reading his mother's books. After finishing *Muluk al-Arab* (Kings of the Arabs) and *al-Bukhalaa'* (Avarice and the Avaricious) in Paris, at his new place of residence he began familiarizing himself with classical Arabic poetry, which had been one of his father's main sources for understanding the world and its affairs.

Mathilde encompassed him with every care, shared his room sometimes, though she never invited him to her place. She told him about her grandfather and how he'd converted the French "bourgeois" home into a hotel, how he added a second story and bought the garden behind it and annexed it to it. The house was owned by her father and his brother, who traveled to New York and never returned. He sent just one long letter that her father used to read to them from time to time. In it he declared his permanent severance of his relationship with his family in France and with the old European continent after having discovered freedom and true equality in America, as he said. People said he had been living with a beautiful woman much younger than him who hailed from one of those places in the Middle East and that she ended up inheriting everything he owned in New York and all the goods he used to sell, before taking it all back with her to her country.

During World War II, German soldiers turned the hotel into a command center when their military occupation spread to the south of France. Several movies were filmed in it afterward, and it hosted some artists who'd been drawn to it by the enchanting light in those Mediterranean parts. Her father would let them stay for free in exchange for portraits they painted of his only daughter Mathilde. And that was how she accumulated no less than twenty portraits of her in watercolors, charcoal, and pastels, and even an oil painting depicting her sitting on the garden swing.

It would occur to Zakariya as he strolled with her and she spoke with brevity and ambiguity about her early marriage and subsequent divorce, and about her admiration of Paul Valéry and her attachment to her son Jean Baptiste, and after that her belief that she had met the man that she had always hoped for without knowing who he was…it occurred to him that he was living inside a bubble guarded by fate. He liked to believe that the credit for that went to his mother Emily and all her prayers, so he sent her a letter—at that period at the end of the epoch of handwritten letters—in which he told her he was making inquiries about the best way to learn about wine making as he'd promised her before he left, and that now he was staying at a beautiful place with nice people. "Nothing in the world can take the place of your love and Marta's love and my longing for my homeland, but it is the first time since I left that I feel I could actually settle here…" He hesitated a moment before adding, "…at least for a good while." Before the letter arrived at his house on the slope of Mount Lebanon, before the mailman handed it to his sister Marta who rushed to open it even before seeing her mother's name on it, Zakariya learned of Mathilde Lagrange's illness.

Months earlier he had started seeing dark spots on her belly and her back, and noticed how she insisted on turning off all the lights until it was nearly pitch black between them, claiming, unconvincingly, something about privacy. And after making love she would hurry to put her clothes back on and cover up. He didn't ask her why, believing it was some natural "imperfection" of hers. And he also noticed the alternation of her moods between times of exuberance, when words and laughter gushed out of her, and moments of shrinking back and being silent, when her body would collapse into the chair and her eyes would wander.

He found out from Jerome. Mathilde was late; she didn't come back at the expected time. So Zakariya asked the sixty-year-old Jerome, who was not stingy with his answer. Rather, he acted as though he'd been waiting for the question so he could tell him that Mathilde had been going to the University Hospital in Marseille for chemotherapy twice a month. She had blood cancer—leukemia—and sometimes she was overly exhausted after the treatment and preferred to stay out of sight at her aunt's in Marseille until she regained her strength.

Zakariya's entire world shook. His bubble burst. It was all over for him, but he held on. He didn't scream. He tried to camouflage his feelings and asked Jerome, "Are you a relative?"

"No, but I spent my life in this hotel. I started with her father in the fifties. He was a great man who joined the French Resistance during the war."

Mathilde returned from Marseille. She was just as he always knew her to be, but he couldn't hide his bewildered eyes from her.

"Did Jerome tell you?"

"Yes."

"I asked him to tell you."

"But I'm the one who asked him about you."

"He was going to find a way to tell you."

"Why?"

95

"To free you from me. Now you can pack your bags and leave for some other life. You shouldn't be deprived of another life you deserve that's better than this one."

Tears glistened in his eyes as he hugged her close to his heart for a long time.

She added, while also crying in her turn, "And because I'm going to lose my hair from the treatment and put on a silly wig and I won't have any desire for a period of time and after that I'll either die or get my energy back."

Between one hour and the next, Zakariya's feelings of tenderness crowded out his feelings of desire. He would no longer crave her after that day, despite their continuing to meet in his bed. His outward concern for her increased, as did his endeavoring not to go overboard with concern so as not to remind her with every kind act that he was tending to a sick girlfriend. The color of the days they spent together changed, turned gray, and then *The Blue Violinist* suddenly appeared.

A medium-sized oil painting inside a fancy wooden frame that Mathilde had stood up on the couch one afternoon and propped against the wall. They sat down, side by side, and started pondering it. The largest portion of the canvas was taken up by a man much like a clown in his colorful patchwork clothing and his funny hat, suspended at night in a clear sky above the rooftops of a poor village as he played a small violin with a bird standing on his shoulder and another on his thigh, the moon over him and a bouquet of heavenly flowers to his right.

She knew the painting's artist, Marc Chagall, and had visited with him on several occasions. He'd told her about his humble childhood, about his father who didn't want him to be an artist. His religion prohibited him from depicting God's creations. He had come to the west and died an old man in a house above the highlands that he bought in Saint-Paul-de-Vence. He frequented The Sunflower and liked to sit in the garden with his wife, and that's where, one day, for no stated reason, he'd brought that painting to her parents. They asked only that her parents take care of the violinist, for he was the sad musician of his village in White Russia. He would play on holidays and would hold out his hat to receive a few meager coins.

"Why did he call it *The Blue Violinist* when there's no blue in the painting except a small spot in the middle of the bouquet of flowers?"

She had asked him that same question, and he said that the title should not summarize the work. "The work summarizes itself. No need to be redundant."

Zakariya shrugged his shoulders unconvinced, and Mathilde picked up the painting and gave it to him. "I want you to take it to your room and hang it on the wall across from your bed so you can discover that a painting's beauty is gauged by our ability to bear seeing it fixed before our eyes for a long time."

Whenever Zakariya lay on his bed he would ponder *The Violinist* and delve into the details that appeared around the musician. Then he would withdraw from it and ponder his situation with Mathilde. The role of lover began to fade gradually, and he felt that the scenario with women—falling in love and then abandoning them—was recurring with him once again. Every time he felt his presence had become critical with respect to the woman he was involved with, the world came crashing down on him. He became suffocated. He counted himself among the persecuted and began looking for a chance to get out. But Mathilde's illness stood as an obstacle to his escape. He wouldn't leave her and take off; he wanted her to recover completely, to regain her spirits, and perhaps for her to be the one to distance herself so he could finally reach the point of making a surprise departure. But he was incapable of carrying out such a ploy.

He kept track of the lab results and went with her more than once to the hospital in Marseille. He'd take her in the Citroën, seated by his side. The lust for words between them waned. Half the way was spent in total silence. They'd talk about the weather forecast like a couple of retirees. She'd turn the radio on sometimes feeling afraid of the emptiness. Finally, the series of chemotherapy treatments was completed, and the results afterward were positive, but the doctor didn't hide the fact that there was still a chance the cancer would come back; statistics pointed to as much. Zakariya lasted another month. His joy during that time over Mathilde's having restored her health and her beauty was an honest joy. It was difficult to predict that the reason for his wide smile every time he saw her and his kisses that had regained some of their passion, was the fact that his hour of escape had drawn near.

She went with Jean Baptiste to Morocco for the weekend. This time, instead of the brassiere or the golden brooch, Zakariya Mubarak chose to steal "The Blue Violinist." He packed his bag and took off at dawn's first light. He didn't notice Jerome. On his night watch, Jerome was not surprised to see Zakariya fleeing as he monitored his steps and had been following him from the moment he'd heard the old elevator operating at such an unusual hour. He stepped toward the entrance door and saw the way Zakariya looked all around the deserted square as he loaded his things, started the Citroën, and departed from Saint-Paul-de-Vence, just as he had arrived on a clear spring day two years earlier.

Zakariya preferred running away in nice weather.

After fleeing Saint-Paul-de-Vence, Zakariya fasted from women. He needed a prolonged convalescence from the physical effort of satisfying them and confessing his passion to them. He enjoyed living by himself in a spacious studio and on a spacious bed where he could spread out his things. Free to lie down or get up whenever he liked, spend his days as he liked, listen to his music, read his newspapers. He wore the two colors that appealed to him—black and white—along with the red ribbon of his Panama hat. He took his time shopping with a wicker basket in hand from the roaming vegetable and cheese vendors, and went back home to eat his own creations in the kitchen. He savored afternoon naps and finished reading the Arabic selections from Abu Hayyan al-Tawhidi in his *Kitaab al-Imtaa' wa-l-Muaanasa* (Book of Enjoyment and Bonhomie) to Mikhael Naimeh in his *Saba'un* (Seventy). He traveled carrying his life's belongings in a single suitcase; in the other hand he waved around the valuable metal tube, to which he had attached a carrying strap, and he would sling it up onto his shoulder like a hunting rifle. He'd choose a train that stopped in every village and every station, the omnibus that was taken by humble, mild-tempered passengers not trying to beat the clock. He'd get off at stops whose names inspired him or whose buildings beckoned to him or where he'd glimpse a shadow— of a woman or a man—that cast an air of secrecy on the place. He'd sit on old stone bridges, sip black coffee in small squares, go inside cathedrals and listen to the big pipe organ and to the choir chanting "Glory to God in the highest and on earth peace." He stood for half an hour inside the Louvre in front of Géricault's *Raft of Medusa*, convinced that that group of drowning victims being pummeled by storms from every direction summarized the fate of all humankind. He ate coq au vin and learned how to make it himself. He waited for the tide to rise in the gulf of Mont Saint

Michel and danced the waltz to oboe music in commemoration of the fall of the Bastille in a remote village in Lower Normandy.

The few times when he spoke to his mother and sister, he felt things there were the same as ever. Emily's voice was faint, and the words that came out of her mouth with difficulty constantly betrayed the fact that she was standing over the abyss of her melancholy soul. His sister Marta made up for the lack of words, teasing him about the marriage he was always putting off. He'd respond with a double dose of the same back at her and could hear Raheel making noise in the background, clamoring for the phone while no one granted her request.

After enough time elapsed to atone for his betrayals of women and his cruel abandonment of Mathilde Lagrange, Zakariya Mubarak returned to his old self. He started paying attention again to those lost women passing through. He recognized them from the look in their eyes, in public parks or taverns. He'd hit on the one sitting alone reading, knowing that she was ready to trade her thick book for a man who could keep her company and alleviate her loneliness, even if with a few deceitful, carefully worked out words she knew were deceitful and carefully worked out. Women for a night or two, of all ages, whose names he never asked and who left nothing behind but a mysterious scent of perfume, an earring that had fallen off inadvertently, or a stick of lipstick he'd snatched from the edge of the bathroom sink. He made them happy, made them laugh with anecdotes he'd heard here and there. He'd make them red beet salad with ginger and pine nuts or grilled camembert cheese with dried apricots and olives before claiming he had to go away the next morning, waving a train ticket in his hand that had expired months earlier, so he could regain his freedom, his physical independence, if only for a short time.

He'd journey east, toward the French-German borders. He'd climb the Château du Haut-Kœnigsbourg, which was so high it seemed to have been built by *jinns,* and then hike down into the valley of Saint Odile. He traveled the wine route and joined a tour around the vineyard near Strasbourg. He wanted to finish what his father had begun but failed to achieve. Everything he knew about grapes he'd learned from his father Ibrahim—the difference between the taste of the *Marini* and the seedless *Zeini* variety, and between the *Merwah* and the *Shami* variety that doesn't get sweet until the end of October. He had come there to learn how to cultivate his family's orchard and plant it with Reisling vines, which had yet to make their way to the shores of the Mediterranean, and make incomparable white wine from them.

But he didn't see it through. He wandered through the Black Forest as part of an organized tourist trip, and fate struck him with a young woman, one of the ones he'd claimed at one time would never make his heart skip a beat. Just like that—at the peak of his period of frivolity, of turning encounters with women into mere sexual play and prattle, one day focused on the majesty of the world and the next on its triviality, successive exercises in seduction involving a mix of suggestive glances and pick-up lines, which had brought him to the point of ruin—just like that he met her, and she made him lose all control of his life.

She was five feet, four inches tall and weighed one hundred twenty pounds. She wore size thirty-six shoes. He sat down beside her in one of the seats at the back of the bus. Her shiny black hair and pink dress with white polka dots reminded him of the old Hollywood actresses. He tried to think of a good name to give her until he woke up the next dawn muttering, "Vivien Leigh. She's Vivien Leigh." She caught him completely by surprise.

For days he resisted his attraction to her. A voice deep down inside him tried to warn him not to slip, but he didn't listen. He braced himself, avoided meeting up with her one time, and then when evening fell, he couldn't help himself from going after her in the hotel. He, the women expert, lost his eloquence. The truth of his feelings made him tongue-tied. He couldn't finish a sentence and looked idiotic with his hand shaking as he handed her a cup of coffee. He, who believed he had consumed all love's emotions and had drawn up a list of all the women he'd won over in his life and then tore it up in shame, discovered inside himself this incredible attraction that had come out of nowhere!

One of the last days of the trip, they were strolling through Strasbourg Cathedral Square and the conclusion of their conversation in English went like this:

"I'm going back to Boston, and I don't know what to expect there."

"Tomorrow?"

"Yes."

"Would you give me a few days to get a U.S. entry visa?"

"I don't advise you to come with me...I'm not a good person to get involved with."

"Who said I was looking for peace of mind?"

"One can say I warned you, at least."

Then she looked deeply at his face. She stood on tiptoes to remove the hat from his head, put it on her own head, and then walked in front of him wiggling her little butt.

"I'll wait for you under one condition."

"And what is that?"

"That I have a child with you."

"I don't like children, but I like you."

"That's nonsense. I say to you here in front of this church...

Who is the Saint here?"

"The Holy Virgin."

"I bet that you will love your child and you won't love me, and that you will try to control me. You're depraved like all men, but I will take a chance on you. I believe life is a series of crashing into walls, and this is one of them. Where are you from?"

"From Lebanon."

"What's your name?"

"Zakariya."

She shrugged her shoulders as a sign of her indifference.

He went with her.

He moved for six years to another planet. Life defeated him with the crushing blow there, and then he went back home.

First, he went back to Paris.

Bad dreams hounded him, the kind that tore out his insides. He'd lift his head when he woke up in the morning from a pillow drenched with the tears he'd cried in his sleep—if he managed to find a way to fall asleep. He lost track of which day of the week it was, forgot names of people and places, stayed all alone in a sad hotel room that shook with the subway passing beneath it and overlooked a dark wall in the tenth arrondissement. He didn't bathe, didn't shave, ate very little, ate in spite of himself, couldn't read, couldn't concentrate. He'd curl up in bed, in fetal position, pull the covers over his head, and flee from the images that besieged him. He ended his story with women once and for all.

He wandered through the boulevards of the Right Bank of the Seine, crowded with pedestrians of all types. Sometimes he'd carry the glass bottle of ashes with him and talk to himself, and from time to time, he'd stop his train of thought and memories with a sharp sound he would release in agony toward the sky. He would scream about his inability to do anything or would blame himself for actions that were no longer possible to take. And in the brief and rare moments of his "optimism," and if he had any will remaining, he would make plans to sell *The Violinist* so he could use the money to plant French grapevines there in his hometown, in Mahmoudiya Orchard, and name his wine *Mary*.

He put himself together one day and went to see the Albino. The Albino was his enemy, but Zakariya believed he deserved the punishment the Albino had given him and didn't know anyone in Paris with as much clout, whose language he spoke, and whose tricks he could see through. And at their last encounter, he'd glimpsed some fondness in the Albino's eyes amid his hot anger over his wife's infidelity. In any case, Zakariya Mubarak no longer feared taking risks but rather sought them out.

His assumption turned out to be correct when the owner of *Le Cèdre du Liban* gave him an unexpected warm welcome as he came through the front door of the restaurant there on François the 1st Street. He welcomed the man he'd nicknamed the Prodigal Son with three kisses on the cheeks, as if nothing had happened between them. He was pleasant, ordered him an iced mint drink, and expressed his concern after noticing a slouch in Zakariya's step, fatigue engraved on his face, and his flat refusal to have some lunch.

"You seem like you're in rough shape. What did you do to yourself, man?"

Zakariya responded with philosophical brevity, "Such is life, my friend!"

The Albino had another explanation, which he summarized, smiling.

"The ladies killed you, as far as I can tell."

He said it remembering the charming restaurant manager whose love the beautiful mature women used to vie for. Zakariya shook his head but added, like someone mocking himself, "No, just one lady killed me, who was barely six years old!"

He swallowed hard, turned his face away. The tears would have started spilling from his eyes if the Albino hadn't taken pity on him and changed the subject. He started praising Zakariya's restaurant management skills, his efficiency, his integrity. And in an attempt to make up for how things had ended up between them, the Albino showered a flood of insults in Arabic onto his ex-wife that extended to all foreign women, that is all non-Lebanese women. It was as if with this attack, he was taking vengeance on Zakariya's behalf for the wretchedness of that western Eve that he didn't bother to inquire about. It became clear from his harping about his wife that she had stolen money from him, thousands of euros, and sent it to her family in Argentina. No sooner would he turn his back than she would open her legs to the first passerby. The local policeman or the driving instructor. So, he divorced her and rid himself of her. He ended his epic by saying, "I'd rather have chaff from my own country than wheat from a foreigner!"

Zakariya relaxed a little. The dancing around the subject didn't go on for long; he didn't have the strength for it. He told the Albino about the oil painting he had in his possession and how he didn't trust anyone with it but him.

"It's worth a lot," he told him.

"Where is it?"

"In a safe place."

"And what do you mean by 'a lot,' my friend?"

"Millions of euros…"

He wrapped his arms around Zakariya's shoulder.

"Are you kidding me?"

There was a look of audacity with unforeseen consequences in Zakariya's eyes that made the Albino regard him with interest. Zakariya wrote down on a slip of paper the name of the artist, the title of the painting, its measurements, and date of production. He had no ability and no desire to speak. "Check for yourself. The painter is one of the most famous artists. We'll talk later."

"And how did you get it?"

"Some women bring ruin, and some bring fortune!"

The Albino laughed out loud, which seemed a promising sign to Zakariya, and so he started the countdown to his homeward voyage. He spoke to Marta, and she tried to convince him to postpone it, but he refused to listen.

He remained convinced that his soul would not be still anywhere except Tel Safra.

The Albino called him back two days later.

"I have a buyer for you…"

It was conventional to obscure things in those circles, especially since the buyer was most likely the Albino himself.

"…but you have to trust me on this."

The Albino wanted to meet with an art expert first.

"I don't buy fish swimming in their own sea."

The expert, who spoke French with a strange accent, showed special interest in the certificate signed by Marc Chagall himself that indicated the date of production and size of the painting. Mathilde had given it to Zakariya the day she gave him the painting to keep in his room at the Sunflower as though she expected there to be some doubt about its authenticity.

The expert did not trust Zakariya. He'd approach *The Blue Violinist* and back away from it, approach it and back away from it, gently brush his fingers over the surface of the painting. After the first stage of exploration, he pulled out a magnifying glass from his pocket—a loupe that attaches to the eye like the ones watch repairmen use—and focused on the violinist's face and the bird standing on his shoulder. He did what he thought "experts" do before pieces of art so as to examine the artist's brushstroke. He shook his head like a pendulum and gave the Albino looks with obvious meaning. After Zakariya went out carrying the painting and the artist's certificate, he stepped aside with the Albino who had already begun making business maneuvers. "It looks like a child's painting. I don't see why it's priced so high."

Zakariya had nothing to say, and he didn't even inquire about the expert's opinion.

"Is it true the artist is Jewish?" the Albino asked.

"Yes, I think so. He was originally from White Russia."

The Albino stuck out his bottom lip; his suspicions about some matter had been confirmed.

They agreed that Zakariya should hold onto the painting, take good care of it, and carry it with his bags to Lebanon. Then delivery and payment could take place in his hometown which was close to the capital.

"These things are complicated in France."

The Albino's attention was drawn to Zakariya's silence during the discussion and his staring into space, and then his suddenly saying, as though emerging from a deep train of thought that had led him to this conclusion, "Can you sell me a gun?"

The Albino laughed but didn't seem reassured by Zakariya's request after Zakariya added, to calm things, that he wanted it to protect himself while he had this "fortune" in his hands.

"You want it here?"

"No. There."

The Albino promised to get it to him there and added as a

sort of appreciation gift for buying the painting, "Consider the gun my gift to you. It'll be delivered to your door."

They also agreed to stay in touch via text messages rather than direct phone calls for the sake of secrecy. And before they separated, the Albino stuck his index finger in the air.

"What's this?" asked Zakariya.

"One million."

"One million what?"

"One million U.S. dollars."

Zakariya put three fingers up and said, "Go to Google and search on Chagall and Christie's and behold a big surprise."

The Albino understood. He put two fingers up and said, "You're going to be rich, son of Mubarak, but don't you dare play any tricks on me!"

Zakariya felt that the Albino's behavior betrayed a lack of seriousness. He no longer put much faith in the success of the operation. A faint smile appeared on his face as he said his good-byes and walked away.

10

Assistant Investigating Judge Kamal Abu Khalid asked Marta to show him to Zakariya's room before agreeing to the coffee she served him, which was heavy on the cardamom, the way she liked it. Dressed in black, a color that brought out her beauty, Marta continued counting her brother's many virtues while also harping on her original accusation. "People told me that my despicable cousins were here in town the day he was killed."

Kamal gestured toward Raheel, so Marta whispered to him that her aunt didn't understand what they were saying and that she'd been ill from birth. "But I swear, we'll all be dead, and she'll still be here all by herself!"

"And are these 'people' willing to testify in court?"

"They didn't see my two cousins themselves, but other people told them that they zipped through town Sunday afternoon in a white Mercedes."

"Villages are always teeming with rumors."

The investigating judge found a welcome opportunity to teach

Marta a practical lesson. "Your uncle Younis's sons, if they wanted to kill your brother Zakariya, and even if they succeeded in killing you yourself and your aunt after that, then they still wouldn't get any inheritance. And they know that because they consulted lawyers. They were only threatening you so you would cave in and voluntarily give them a share of the house and the orchard and money as compensation for being left out of the inheritance."

"Didn't they tell you about our great-grandmother Philomena and what she brought back with her from New York?"

"No, they didn't tell me, and quit going all over the place."

The strange things kept piling up one after the other, and Marta was not the easiest riddle to solve. Kamal Abu Khalid tried to catch her off guard. "After Zakariya returned from abroad, did a stranger, someone you don't know, come to see you?"

She started naming the few people who had stepped across the threshold that summer to welcome Zakariya, adding some criticism for the mayor, who neglected public affairs, and some praise for the Nabhan family, who were some of the Druze residents of the town that were good at performing "social obligations." She stopped all of a sudden.

"Yes, a man I didn't know came; he wasn't from here. He came in a black Range Rover, with tinted windows. He had another young man with him who waited for him outside, gazing out at the distant sea as if seeing it for the first time. He refused to come inside despite Zakariya's insistence."

Her brother introduced the visitor to her in a loud voice. She got the feeling Zakariya raised his voice so she wouldn't forget the name.

"Badih Makhlouf, the kingpin of the Mar Mikhael area of Beirut."

Makhlouf, a graduate of the militia ranks as they'd come to

112

call it, felt that no one else had his level of clout in the streets of the capital, where he'd fought. With the cessation of hostilities and the return of night life to the capital, he started parking cars for patrons of one of the restaurants in the side streets for a small fee. Then he expanded his influence and took charge of an entire "Valet Parking" operation. He hired dozens of young men in the booming nightclub district. And he'd sell firearms to the rich patrons, all the latest models: Smith & Wesson revolvers that the young men carried with pride, or even small Beretta automatic rifles. They needed them for self-defense with the rise in kidnappings and muggings at night or on the mountain roads.

Kamal asked her to repeat the name so he could record it on his phone.

"They had coffee right here just like we are doing now," she added. "They spoke in generalities. Badih talked, actually, and Zakariya listened. I can't forget all the noise Aunt Raheel was making, how perturbed she was by that man's presence. We know her well. She has a sixth sense about people. She didn't like him, but he was friendly and respectable. After a little while, Zakariya winked at him and they went into his bedroom, locking the door behind them."

"Did you hear the conversation?"

She tried to say no, with her eyes simultaneously betraying the opposite.

"Don't try to deceive me. You were listening behind the door."

"He gave Zakariya something, even though he'd come in empty-handed, and told him it was a gift from the Albino."

"Who?"

"The Albino."

The investigator wrote the name down.

After that, she'd heard a metal screeching sound and warnings to her brother to be careful. Then they spoke at length about some matter she didn't understand.

"Why are you lying to the investigator? Did they discuss a painting? An oil painting?"

She was surprised by the question.

"Yes. How did you know?"

"They pay me a salary to know. When did Badih Makhlouf visit you?"

"A month after Zakariya came back."

The investigator was pursuing his line of interrogation.

"What was your brother holding in his hands the day he left the house, before he was killed?"

Her answers were ready, as if she'd been expecting the questions.

"I don't know. I went to the butcher shop in the town square, and then I stopped in for a visit at one of my relatives'. When I came back, Zakariya wasn't home. If only he'd stayed behind a little longer, maybe his fate would have turned out differently."

Her eyes welled up all over again.

He wasn't going to be dragged in by her. He went into Zakariya's room and locked the door behind him, too.

The room was neat and tidy. Zakariya was used to living alone. A bed, a closet, a table and chair, two suitcases; the frugality of a hotel room. The investigating judge lifted the mattress to peek under it and found some old movie posters. He looked under the bed, opened the two suitcases and the closet, and all the drawers. Nothing caught his attention except two men's hats, a collection of wine bottles, some women's keepsakes, some dolls, a colorful wooden Pinocchio, and a big bear made of pink fabric. He stood in the middle of the room and scanned it one last time. On the night table beside the bed, he noticed a book with a letter on top of it and a dark glass bottle next to it with "Mary" written on it. He remembered that the name Mary had come up in one of the text messages.

On his way out, he asked Marta who Mary was. She said she didn't know and that as far as she knew her brother had fallen in love with lots of women. He took the book and the letter with him and left the bottle on the table. He wasn't going to find anything else of interest, and he wasn't going to find *The Blue Violinist*...

The moment he got back to his office, the investigating judge told the district police to bring in Badih Makhlouf. Kamal Abu Khalid preferred to interrogate sternly and unemotionally, to put the witness face-to-face with the truth.

He made it clear to Makhlouf, the moment he entered, that he was in no position to refuse to cooperate with the investigation. The police knew that he sold weapons and other contraband in the night clubs, and it would be easy to go after him legally, put him in jail, and bring in witnesses who could testify against him.

Makhlouf was of strong build, had white hair and a black moustache. He promised to tell him everything he knew. Kamal Abu Khalid looked him over, trying to detect the killer within him.

"Who is Zakariya Mubarak?"

He began hesitantly. He mentioned a favor requested by an old friend of his living in Paris.

The inspector stared at a sheet of paper in front of him.

"The Albino?"

"Yes. We were all part of the same group that protected the gold market in the commercial center when the fighting broke out in the mid-seventies."

"And what was the favor?"

"To give Zakariya Mubarak a new gun per his request. I brought it to him in his hometown, and that's all that happened between us."

"No, that's not all that happened between you. Another thing happened—the man was found murdered in the town's vicinity a few days ago."

Makhlouf started screaming theatrically and his eyes widened. But the surprised look on his face did not appear to be feigned.

"And the matter didn't end there. The painting has vanished, and you have knowledge of the painting. Don't try to evade the issue because I know a lot of things. We, no, just you, are looking at premeditated murder with aggravated robbery! With any luck, you'll only get hard labor for life, because the state doesn't condone the death sentence under the country's current situation."

Badih Makhlouf didn't need all those threats to get him to cooperate with the investigation. He tried to spill his guts in all honesty and in chronological order.

"At the beginning of the summer, the Albino called me from Paris, and we talked for about half an hour on the phone until my ear got hot. He was all excited and told me about that painting and how much it was worth and that he'd found a buyer in Paris. He asked me to go get it. He told me about Zakariya, that he was suffering from some sort of trauma and that it would be easy to do business with him…"

"…Or to compel him by force," the investigating judge interrupted him. "And if he resisted, finish him. That's why you took another man along when you went to visit him, right?" he said, finishing the Albino's train of thought.

"No, not at all. I am not in the business of committing crimes. When I went to his house, I only tried to get him to let me see the painting with my own eyes, that's all, to make sure it was there. But he was smarter than me. He was sad but he wasn't naïve. He asked to see the money first. Two million dollars, he said, just like the Albino had promised me from Paris. How was I supposed to bring him two million dollars? The Albino didn't send a single dollar, and I still haven't even gotten the money he owes me for the gun I gave to Zakariya. But he called me back from Paris to say we could split a huge fortune if we could get hold of that painting. And he said a French art expert verified how much it was worth, so I was talking to Zakariya, pretending that the Albino had supplied me with the money, and all that was left for us to do was make the exchange. But he insisted on seeing the money first, and after a while he stopped answering my calls. Maybe he felt like we weren't going to pay him anything. He wasn't stupid."

"Who killed him?"

"When was he killed?" Badih Makhlouf asked. He had clearly exerted a lot of effort to tell the truth in all its details.

"Sunday. Ten days ago."

"I tried calling him two or three times that day, but he didn't answer. I even tried to call him yesterday. You can check my phone or his phone to confirm it."

Kamal Abu Khalid didn't show him any courtesy.

"And if I were to check, is that your proof that you're innocent?"

Badih Makhlouf put his head between his hands and bent down to think. When he raised his head, he had tears in his eyes. He told the inspector that he had survived the war. He survived by a miracle in one of the battles in the heart of Bechara El-Khoury Boulevard. An anti-tank missile exploded five meters away from him and killed one of his friends, an only child, twenty years old. He didn't want to go back to those problems.

117

He had a beautiful family, he was building a house for himself in the mountains, and he had a daughter about to enter the university to study law next September. He carried out all his gun sales with the full knowledge of the National Security Bureau. He informed them of every weapon and the name of every buyer.

"I don't want to go to jail."

The investigating judge quit listening. He didn't like to get caught up in emotions. He called in a transcriber to record Badih Makhlouf's answers to a series of questions:

- The Albino's full name, place of birth, occupation, and what illegal activities he might be carrying out in Paris.

- The model of the gun that you gave to Zakariya and how you got it.

- Your whereabouts the Sunday the crime was committed, especially in the hours after noon, and the names of witnesses—other than relatives—who can confirm where you were.

- Is it possible, in your opinion, that the Albino hired some other person to do the job?

- If Zakariya Mubarak had agreed to show you the Chagall painting, what would you have done?

Only the last question was disconcerting.

"I don't know, but now I'm glad he didn't do as I asked," Badih Makhlouf said after giving it some thought.

It seemed an honest answer to Kamal Abu Khalid, who wasn't going to give up on the idea that the painting had been the motive for the murder. Before leaving his office, he caught sight of the book and the letter he'd left on his desk, so he picked them up and took them home with him. The day had been long and tiring, and when he stretched out in front of the television patting the bulldog, which was the position that gave him a feeling of confidence in spite of the shaky evidence, he noticed the book's title, *Usfour min al-Sharq* (A Bird from the East) by Tawfiq al-Hakim, and read a couple of pages. He nearly fell asleep before discovering a new surprise in the letter that just might bring matters full circle.

My Dear Friend Zakariya,

The 'train of advancements in technology' left the station without me, so I have yet to enter the world of electronic messaging and still prefer writing by hand, with a pen and paper of my own choosing. I remember your stay at the Sunflower fondly, and likewise all the staff here hold you in high esteem. Special regards to you from Jean Baptiste.

The truth is, Mrs. Mathilde—who remains in good health after her successful treatment—gave me your mailing address in Lebanon and asked me to write these lines to you, which I hope will not cause you any grief. First, maybe you have hung the Chagall painting in your room and are enjoying looking at it, which would be the best thing you could have done, or maybe you've sold it, and that would be where the problem lies, because you should know that The Blue

Violinist is a forgery painted by a talented artist, and the certificate of authenticity is a forgery, too. Mrs. Mathilde does not know Marc Chagall and he never stepped foot in the Sunflower Hotel. In brief, that was all a test for you and for your true feelings. She wanted your betrayal of her to be for a respectable sum of money, not just the promise of a little. You see, the painting that you took—and I saw you carrying it, along with your luggage—if it were authentic might be worth 20 million U.S. dollars. She used that same test before, with a painting by Matisse and another by Nicolas de Staël, on two other men who couldn't resist the temptation. Mathilde has decided to spend the rest of her days with the art forger, who she found to be more "genuine" than those lovers of hers who disappeared under the cloak of darkness.

With my sincere regards, and regrets from Mathilde who says that her leukemia was actually authentic.

Signed,
Jerome Guidoni
Night Watchman, Sunflower Hotel
Saint-Paul-de-Vence, August 15

According to the postmark, the letter reached Tel Safra one month before Zakariya Mubarak's murder. In other words, it had taken three weeks for it to cross the Mediterranean Sea. Although it tore Kamal Abu Khalid's murder theory to shreds, it didn't take away any of his resolve. He had to find that painting, or rather that forgery, so he could piece together a complete picture of the events. He shouldn't settle for Badih Makhlouf's claims of innocence. He could be a shrewd actor. He was a man of experience who "wasn't born yesterday." He'd come so close to death that dealing with life's concerns had become easy for him. And maybe the Albino sent in a substitute for Makhlouf to kill Zakariya Mubarak, and maybe he'd lured him to the pine grove to make the exchange, taken possession of the promised Marc Chagall painting without giving him any money, before discovering it was worthless because he, of course, hadn't read the letter. The absence of Mathilde Lagrange's gift kept that supposition alive. And above all that, doubts about the validity of the night watchman's letter remained stuck in Kamal Abu Khalid's mind, and about how the letter got to Tel Safra. One could not eliminate the possibility that the letter was an additional deception, another forged document, in the game of lies that was being played by Mathilde, the French hotel owner, whose picture he failed to find in Zakariya's phone.

He could not back off, for all eyes were on him, and the public prosecutor was counting on him, too. He was reviewing the details of the investigation when Marta Mubarak's recent "antics" suddenly popped into his mind—as he was going out onto the patio after locking the door to Zakariya's room carrying the book and the letter, and warning Marta not to enter the room because it was essential to the investigation, while Raheel fidgeted on her couch and incessantly repeated, "Druze, Druze, Druze..."

He had looked to Marta, who volunteered an explanation.

"She loves her nephews—her brother Younis's sons and wants to clear them of Zakariya's murder!"

Kamal got fed up with Marta and raised his voice.

"But what is she saying now?"

"She's suggesting that the Druze..."

Mubarak's town witnessed a century and a half ago. However, the farmers, especially the Christians among them who suffered defeat at the time, made sure to pass down the various chapters of their struggle to their children orally, from one generation to the next. Voices from the heart of the tragedy bear witness to the sufferings of individuals, which are of little consequence to historians more interested in narrating their "spin" on the events than in recording their actual details.

One of those hushed and concealed voices was that of Bahiya al-Murad. After washing her daughter Philomena's hair and braiding her two pigtails, she would take her by the hand, walk her down to the overlook at the edge of the pine grove, and start talking. Mostly when she spoke it was as though she were talking to herself. She chose to entrust Philomena with the safekeeping of the tragedy of her life. She saw in the eyes of her eldest daughter what she did not see in the face of Philomena's innocent younger sister Katarina. Bahiya would start talking where Philomena could hear her, and Philomena would listen. Though still at an age when the meanings of some things were difficult for her, her mother's deep sorrow found its way into her young heart, along with that anger of hers that no amount of time could extinguish. Bahiya told her how beautiful the old days had been, how bountiful and prosperous. They had lived a life of ease and comfort, because her father was a business partner with the Abi Nakad family in the Mahmoudiya Orchard.

"You see it there before you. It goes all the way down to the bottom of the valley."

He had uprooted the ancient olive trees and planted mulberry trees in their place, in order to raise silkworms. Silk production was very popular at the time, and Bahiya was of marriageable age. Relatives and neighbors sang the praises of her beauty, so a young man from one of the nearby villages came on two occasions to their house for evening gatherings. He was a *zajal* poet-singer who wore a striped vest and red *keffiyeh* made of pure silk: a gallant, well-mannered man. He waited for her a few days later on the road to the village bakery just so he could walk a few short steps with her and tell her in all seriousness and brevity that if she did not accept his marriage proposal then he would enter the order of the Mariamite monks. Her heart would start pounding whenever she caught sight of him in town or at Mahmoudiya Orchard where he worked with her father during silkworm season and otherwise learned the tailoring trade the rest of the year. She persuaded her mother, who consulted with her father, and he in turn consented. Everyone agreed to have the wedding on the Feast Day of Saints Peter and Paul. Bahiya started counting the days as she prepared a trousseau of her own handiwork. But early in May, the townspeople were drawn out from their homes by sounds of shouting and clamor outside. Some peasants were carrying the body of a young man from the town who had been murdered along the cobblestone road to Damascus. He had been traveling with three government soldiers who didn't raise a finger to stop the Druze from beating him with sticks and stoning him to death. The townspeople prayed over him and buried him.

A delegation of the town's Druze community came the next day to condemn the incident and declare they had nothing to do with it. They made an agreement with the Christians not to fight with each other, and that whosoever was bent on causing problems should go join the rest of his faction outside Tel Safra. Tensions were defused. People went back to their work, and Bahiya busied herself once again with preparations for her wedding day, until the news of Sheikh Abu Saeed Hamdan came along.

He was one of Tel Safra's socialites, and a powerful and influential man. He'd fallen prey to an ambush set up for him by the Christians in the Hammana district. It was said that they tortured him before killing him and that one of his assailants was a young man from Tel Safra who wasn't heard from afterward nor were his whereabouts ever known again. The Druze did not react immediately but waited until their messengers got the word to their relatives and supporters in the neighboring villages. They assembled outside the town in the morning, before the church bells for the First Mass rang out; they attacked the Christian quarter and began burning the houses and property. Nayfeh, the sister of Sheikh Abu Saeed, marched at the front of the line, chanting war songs that called for revenge.

Bahiya went outside barefoot, worried about her father and fiancé who had set out for the orchard at dawn. Three or four of the Druze were mounted on horses, while the rest were marching on foot. She raced ahead of them to the orchard and tried to face them off.

"We have never fought with you!" she shouted. "We want peace. Let us be!"

But one of the mounted men charged right at her on his horse and nearly trampled her, causing her to fall down on the side of the road. Her father and fiancé refused to flee like the other Christians who were not in the habit of coming to each other's aid, because they were unorganized and lacked leadership. The moment the two of them got within the crosshairs of the Druze's rifles, they were shot at from multiple directions; they had no chance of survival. They fell in the middle of the mulberry orchard, and all the assailants disappeared in the blink of an eye.

Whenever Bahiya reached this part of her story, she would stop walking, in order to let her pounding heart quiet down so she could bring back the scene and hold it steady in her mind. She would finish the story, hugging her daughter to her chest.

"I was left all alone with my father and my fiancé in the mulberry orchard. The breeze from the sea was cold that morning. The first time I ever kissed my fiancé he was lying dead on the ground. Completely unarmed, he had stood to face them, refusing to leave my father all alone. I embraced my father who had never once in his life embraced me. My mother used to say I was his favorite. He wouldn't sleep all night if I had the slightest fever, but he was embarrassed to hug me.

"I started crawling on my knees and clutching at the soil. I thought I was going to die, too. In fact, I wished I would die. I started rubbing my face in the mud. I rolled my father onto his back, with his face looking up to the sky. I did the same with my fiancé. I clasped their hands across their chests to make them like the angels in heaven as I imagined them. I prepared a spot on the ground between them and lay down on my back like them. I remember hearing birds chirping before I fell unconscious. They got to us around noon. They picked me up and sat me in the shade of a tree. My mouth was full of mud. I didn't see my father or my fiancé. I didn't know where they had taken them. I tried to weep, but the tears burned in my eyes."

French soldiers came to shore from their warships off the Lebanese coast, and life returned to normal in Tel Safra. Bahiya al-Murad remained inconsolable. Her mother thought she might go mad and that the only cure was marriage. They married her off while she was practically unable to speak, to a poor young man who in less than two years' time gave her Philomena and Katarina before falling into Hajal Valley, where they discovered his body two days later. The mule whose back he had fallen off of led them to his corpse after wandering in the streets weighted down with the sacks of flour it was carrying. People said that Bahiya al-Murad did not weep for her husband because she simply could not mourn any more. They didn't even dress her in black out of fear for her life. It was also said that someone had "written" a spell on her, and there were stories about a woman of Turkoman origin who'd married into the town and was envious of Bahiya's beauty. It was as though whoever had "written" a spell on her had done the same to her daughter Philomena, who resembled her with her pretty figure and big eyes.

Their lot in life was beauty and bad luck. But whereas Bahiya had succumbed to her grief, Philomena fought against her fate and ultimately defeated it. She too fell in love with a young man who did not possess many worldly belongings. In winter, he was asked to clean and prune the trees, and at the start of spring to graft the cherry and apple trees. He pocketed a small income with which he could support himself and his wife. One day a representative from the Abi Nakad family came to ask him to clean up the orchard and till it. However, Philomena, whose mother's terror-stricken voice had made its impression on her, begged him not to do it and not to go near Mahmoudiya Orchard. She offered to compensate him with her small savings and what she could get from selling her two gold bracelets that had belonged to her mother.

Mahmoudiya Orchard has been known for a strange story that persists even in our current times. It started with the murder of Philomena's grandfather and her mother's fiancé and their having been buried secretly at the bottom of the orchard, because getting to the Christian cemetery in town had been impossible at the time due to the presence of armed Druze in that direction. In fact, the matter had been concealed even from Bahiya, who had always assumed they'd been laid to rest up in the cemetery.

The authorities punished the Nakad elders for their participation in the attacks and murders. They confiscated their properties, including Mahmoudiya, whose area encompassed over a hundred dunums. It was left neglected, and for years, no one went near it, until the High Authority of the Mount Lebanon district decreed that personal properties were to be returned to their owners, until work got underway to restore them via partnership contracts.

The orchard had withered, and the nearby silk factory had been shut down, so the only thing to do was uproot the mulberry trees and sell them as cheap firewood. Following that came a *mugharasa* contract whereby the lessee earns half ownership once it turns a profit. It was a fifteen-year contract signed by the heirs of Salman Abi Nakad and a Christian partner, who began planting various types of fast-growing trees, while his workers looked after irrigation and cultivation. He promised himself to start reaping a harvest in three years.

During the long-awaited spring season, a hot *khamsin* wind—never known before in those parts—blew in. They said that it had come all the way from the distant Libyan desert. All the blossoms shriveled up and the fruits and branches became worm-infested, causing them to turn black and wither. In less than a week's time, it destroyed years of constant work and tireless effort. All the townspeople came to observe the disaster with their own eyes, the likes of which they had never seen in their lives and for which they could not fathom an explanation. The *murabi*—quarter-partner—complained about his situation to the Abi Nakad family, who sympathized with him and reclaimed the orchard from him without making him pay a penalty for breach of contract.

History repeated itself a few years later. Bahiya looked up

into the heavens and muttered, "How great you are, Oh God!" Then along came another partner, convinced that the problem wasn't with the land but rather with his predecessor who hadn't been good at caring for it or cultivating it. He planted Mahmoudiya with grapevines and watched over them night and day, nurturing, irrigating, and pruning them, until a cold snap hit along with heavy rain, followed by a morning freeze that burned the tender shoots of the *merwah* and *'abeedi* grapes, dashing all the second partner's hopes. After that, the Abi Nakad family couldn't find anyone to make the land profitable for them, neither as a *murabi'* quarter-partner lessee nor as a *mugharis* half-partner lessee. They neglected it and it became overrun with brush. Snakes and moles and wild mulberry bushes whose fruit people were afraid to eat multiplied, to the point that parents warned their children not to go near the orchard.

During that time, Philomena's husband Masoud Mubarak decided to flee. He donned his clean black striped *sirwal* pants, his white shirt, and his tall boots—the only thing of value he had inherited from his father—and walked off with the clippers tucked in his coat as if he was on his way to prune the trees at one of the orchards. He set out and all trace of him was lost forever. He had been silent about it, hadn't divulged the secret of his sudden departure to anyone. It didn't take Philomena's mother Bahiya al-Murad long to follow the departed ones. In her final years, she lost her ability to speak, causing her to sink deep inside herself, and she never came back out. She died just a few days before the birth of her grandson Jibrail.

Philomena realized that if she stayed amid her broken family, there was no power in heaven that could help them, or if she stayed near her husband's relatives, who did not show much concern for her situation, she would find neither sustenance in life nor the least bit of joy. One morning, while she watched her son crawling around on his knees and trying to get her attention so he could grab onto her and stand up on his feet, she decided to fight the death that was on her trail and cast off the heavy burden of grief from her shoulders. Without actually looking out toward the sea, which was hidden from view at the time by a thick white morning haze, she knew her only option was to go far away. It was common in those days for people to travel to America, even for women to go on their own. And so, she went.

During her absence, the Great War took place. There were shortages and people were poverty-stricken. They were terrified by stories that came from the north, from towns in Byblos and Batroun, of people dying of starvation. Mahmoudiya Orchard was still overrun with brush, not bearing a single fruit. So, the townsfolk banded together in the fall to plow it and plant it with wheat in the hopes that it would provide them with enough bread to sustain them. Katarina alone—who raised her sister Philomena's son Jibrail as one of her own children—knew that nothing planted in Mahmoudiya would grow, because blood is heavy, and because there is divine justice in the world. And indeed, when the wheat stalks shot up and the green of the sprouting spring carpeted the entire vast area, the people started hearing news of locusts storming over the slopes of Mount Lebanon. It wasn't long before they arrived and covered the sky, blotting out the sunlight. They devoured everything in sight in a matter of one or two days. Mahmoudiya reverted once again to an arid orchard. Many Druze fled to their relatives in the Hauran region, and the Christians tried to manage despite the shortages and the spread of typhus.

The owners of Mahmoudiya Orchard gave up all hope for it after the war ended and they were unable to find anyone to partner with them in developing it. Its reputation spread to the neighboring villages, and all sorts of stories were concocted about the land being tainted and how it had been the object of the wrath of Astarte, the goddess in whose honor the Roman temple had been constructed.

This type of mythological story had been spread by an orientalist archeologist called Anatol Barthélemy who had come to Lebanon with the French Army. He brought his daughter with him and rented a house in Tel Safra. He began digging around the Roman temple that was located in the town and which he had read about in a book by a German explorer who had made an account the previous century of the ruins of Syria, Lebanon, and Palestine, and all their wonders. It was said that at night and far from view, Barthélemy unearthed a white marble statue of a beautiful woman with the arms broken off, and a stone bust believed to be that of Caracalla, known as Antoninus, along with a number of vessels and earthenware jars in which the ashes of the dead had been stored after their bodies were burned. He shipped everything he'd found to Marseille in the care of the French Army.

He knew Arabic and conversed with the villagers. He would ask them what tales they had heard from their parents and grandparents about the Roman temple, but they could never quench his thirst. Thinking he was all-knowing, some villagers would ask him his opinion concerning the barren Mahmoudiya Orchard. So, he made up a story—because he was convinced that easterners loved stories—about Astarte's lover, a hunter who was attacked by a wild boar while he was carrying his bow and arrows down that slope they call the Mahmoudiya. The boar bit him in the leg, causing him to bleed heavily for a long time before he finally died. And those flowers the Christians call "Blood of Jesus" flowers, the red anemones that appear in abundance in the orchard, were none other than his deep-red blood. Astarte complained about what happened to her to the supreme god, who ruled that nothing would ever grow in the land again, except for the red blood flower that would carpet its surface the first month of every spring. And it became clear later on that this Barthélemy, who journeyed to other archeological sites, had gone around repeating the myth, which gained a lot of popularity north of Beirut, and thus the belief became widespread that the red hue that muddied one of the rivers there every year was none other than the blood of the hunter killed by his prey.

opened the closet with the key he had entrusted to her during the final days of his illness. She hadn't gone near the closet as long as he was still alive. Inside, she found a lot of gold and jewelry, stacks of dollars, and several issues of the French language newspaper *Le Cri du Peuple*, and books by Proudhon and Auguste Blanqui about equality and utopian society, and there were also some letters he'd exchanged with a woman named Elizabeth Dmitriev that started out with addressing the concerns of the revolution and ended up with expressing feelings of passionate love. Lagrange had participated in the Paris Commune and fired weapons from behind barricades. Then he managed to escape outside the capital when it was stormed, and after that he sailed to New York when the surviving rebel soldiers entered and some of his comrades were executed.

Standing before this fortune, Philomena realized that it would now be possible for her to return to her homeland and build a house for herself and her son in Tel Safra, and buy Mahmoudiya Orchard. The thought always crossed her mind whenever her hometown loomed before her and she recalled the image of her mother Bahiya Murad, lying on the ground in the orchard between her father and her fiancé, hearing the chirping of the morning goldfinches before falling unconscious.

And that was what Philomena did. After returning from abroad and while in the midst of carefully managing the construction of a house she wanted to be the biggest and most beautiful in town, Philomena started asking about land for sale in the vicinity. One of the real estate agents in town sensed there was some money to be made, so he approached her to offer his services. He listed off everything he had in his bag for her to buy—"by proxy" from Jirjis al-Bani, who had immigrated to Mexico. No, of course you wouldn't buy property owned by a

Christian. The Shurfa garden—six wooded dunums. No, that's too small. A big piece of land belonging to the Nabhan family, but there are numerous heirs and it would be hard to get it released…The talk went on and on until he'd exhausted all the options, and then Philomena revealed her true desire. "What about Mahmoudiya Orchard—isn't it for sale?"

The agent was shocked.

"What do you want with that? It's a very big piece of land, over a hundred dunums."

"So what if it is?

"It's useless. It's been deserted since before I was born…"

Philomena gave him an advance on his commission and stated that she was prepared to pay for the land in gold. British pounds. So, off the man went, ready to give it his best effort using all his power and years of experience, believing there were all types of people in the world and what doesn't appeal to you yourself might look good in the eyes of another.

He was gone for days making inquiries and eventually discovered that Sheikh Salman Abi Nakad, owner of the land during the events of 1860, and fearing partitioning of ownership, had bequeathed the entirety of Mahmoudiya to his eldest son, which was something he was permitted to do under the laws governing his sect. That son followed the same doctrine as his father and handed down the land to Salman, the oldest of his sons. This new Salman, of little wisdom and enterprise, tried several times to sell it over the years at a very low price, but his mother would never allow that to happen as long as she lived. The real estate agent found him a month after he'd buried his mother. He was single and alone, and his appearance and house furnishings didn't show the slightest hint of richness. So, he negotiated a price. Salman quoted a price that was double the last price he had been offered under negotiations, and Philomena accepted with no further discussion, not wanting to give the Nakadi fellow a chance to change his mind. She met with him only once, paid him the promised gold pounds, and registered the land in the name of her sister Katarina's son for some reason no one knew but her.

The sale remained a secret that Salman kept from his relatives, until Philomena hired someone to clean up the land, plow it, and put up a cross made of oak in the spot where the town priest told her before she voyaged to New York that her grandfather and her mother's fiancé had been secretly buried. Some of the townspeople thought she was declaring the "Christian" nature of the Mahmoudiya, now that she had taken it from its Druze owners. She rebuilt the terraces that had been destroyed and set to work fortifying them, and then she brought a man who reminded her of her husband Masoud to take charge of cultivating the land. He planted the orchard with American apples of a new variety, in addition to the *muwashshah* and *sukkari* varieties, and *koshia* and *ras al-baghl* pears, and all types of cherries, *shami* and *sultani* peaches, sweet pomegranates, almonds, and other things. She put her sister Katarina's son in charge of looking after the interests of the orchard. She trusted his bookkeeping and was very generous with him without telling him that the land was registered in his name. He assumed ownership would naturally be handed down to his cousin, Philomena's only son Jibrail, who for years he'd thought was his brother and who would visit the orchard like a stranger, confirming what his mother used to say about his not caring much for land.

Salman Abi Nakad's brothers and relatives were infuriated when they heard about the deal. The orchard had been registered in the eldest son's name so that he would hold onto it, not sell it to the Christians. They deliberated among themselves, and it became clear to them that the woman who had come back from across the seas was picking the scab off an old wound. The Great War, with all the tragedies it brought to Mount Lebanon, had been responsible for blotting out everything that had come before. But the wife of Masoud Mubarak, who was still missing without a trace, spent that time in New York far away from all the war's horrors. She heard only some echoes of it, and hadn't seen it with her own eyes. Here she was now, coming back after it was all over just to rehash—as the old-timers in the Druze community believed—some old hostilities that no longer crossed anyone's mind.

They saw for themselves how the land that had remained barren for more than sixty years under their family's care, started to bear fruit, as if it wanted to make up for its barrenness all at once. And just as the townsfolk used to come before to see it withered up, now they came to it in the spring to observe how the trees twinkled with the white of the flowers that covered the branches and carpeted the ground, and how Mahmoudiya had turned into a paradise that loaded its bounty onto mules and donkeys from the beginning of summer to the middle of fall, getting it to the vegetable markets in Beirut early in the season. According to quick calculations, she would get back what she paid for the land in the course of no more than ten seasons.

But the Devil had not yet tired of dancing around that orchard. The first torment happened with a man of the Hamdan clan and maybe even a grandson of Sheikh Abu Saeed himself, who had been killed in the events of 1860. The man got up early. He didn't find anything in the house to alleviate his hunger, so he scolded his wife and walked off to his garden where, with his back leaned against the trunk of a tree, he spotted two mules coming from the Mahmoudiya Orchard with crates of apricots and peaches on their backs. He jumped out into the middle of the road and accosted the mule driver.

"Do not cross this path after today," he barked impolitely. "I will let you pass this once but tell Philomena she doesn't have right of way through our property!"

In his excitement and perhaps to push the deal through or for fear that it might break the deal, the real estate agent had dodged informing Philomena that Mahmoudiya Orchard was hemmed in to the west by Hajal Valley and to the south by a rugged rocky peak, and was separated from the public road in the other two directions by properties belonging to the town's Druze. Or maybe he honestly hadn't thought much of it, knowing that it was customary concerning properties in Mount Lebanon to grant ease of access to cultivated lands via a "foot" path for pedestrians or a "hoof" path for mules and donkeys no more than one meter wide.

Interventions by some judicious folks in town led to the allowance of transport of that year's harvest and deferment of securing a road to the landlocked property to the following season. And during that time when it would have been possible to petition the French Magistrate in Baabda Sérail to grant the right of way, Philomena died. Jibrail Mubarak cared nothing for the matter and turned his back on farming for good, dreaming instead of his mother's buried gold that he'd learned of after deciphering the letter she'd written in English. He preferred womanizing and making easy profits from usury. His cousin, Katarina's son, moved to Beirut to join the Lebanese gendarme at the rank of sergeant major in the vice squad that kept tabs on nightclub operations and regulated brothel activities. The orchard became orphaned once again. Then all on its own and in surprising fashion, the devastation was complete when Yahmour Spring, which irrigated

Mahmoudiya and was mentioned on the property deed as legally providing a water source for it, dried up. The truth was that it didn't dry up but rather vanished completely from the face of the earth, overnight, in the middle of September. Some feared that the Hamdans had rerouted the spring that originated on their property, to punish Philomena, which they had no right to do. It became evident after some research into the matter that the water had sunken into the ground, and one could hear it murmuring deep down through a crevice in the ground like others that had opened up repeatedly in other places around town on various occasions. Experts believed that this was due to Tel Safra's location along the fault line that crossed Mount Lebanon from its southern tip all the way north.

And so, the irrigation canals of Mahmoudiya Orchard dried up, and somebody snuck in at night to take down the cross at the bottom of the orchard, which Philomena never told anyone the reason for her having put there. Young boys and passersby took it upon themselves to enjoy whatever few fruits the trees produced the following neglectful season. In that way, after a few years of rest, the Devil's old curse had come back to it for a new reason. Those who were knowledgeable about land said it had become difficult to irrigate it with anything but rainwater and that it would only be good for farming unirrigated plants, grapes and figs topping the list. Grapevines searched out their own water deep underground while figs didn't like a lot of water. The orchard was left to itself once again, and no one came near it except an engineering battalion of the army that had no idea how, during that hot summer, it had happened upon Mahmoudiya as a place to pitch their four tents. Between the tents a pole was erected and a Lebanese flag hoisted on it, and the soldiers started taking measurements and determining positions for obscure military purposes. But the next morning they were forced to sound the trumpet of departure, take down the tents, and pack up everything they'd set up after a night in which no one slept a wink while battling with the various creeping reptiles and pinching gnats and fearing the sting of scorpions.

And so, every year as the spring equinox approached with the gusting of the hot desert winds, fires would break out in the orchard, consuming the desiccated surface, and the neighbors would come to each other's aid if the winds blew the fires toward their gardens and houses. Meanwhile, no one came with an offer to buy it except the son of Salman Abi Nakad, who offered half the price Philomena had paid his father for it years earlier, using its dried up spring as justification. Jibrail Mubarak scoffed at him and said in earshot of his wife as he was seeing the Nakadi fellow to the door, that if he went down to Beirut, he himself would spend the amount the man had offered in two nights. And it was obvious he meant two nights of fooling around with prostitutes. He winked at the man and then put an end to the discussion, saying with an air of finality, "My mother bought that orchard and we forgot all about it!"

Two decades after that brief discussion, and when Ibrahim Bin Jibrail Mubarak graduated with honors from the university with a degree in agricultural engineering, the family started talking about Mahmoudiya again. Emily, a city girl, was the one who suggested to her husband that they go back to the orchard. The couple headed to Mahmoudiya one weekend on foot, both protecting their heads from the sun with hats made of cork like the ones the white missionaries in Africa were known for. They discussed the place's constant exposure to the sun, the character-istics of the clay soil, and the possibility of relying on rainwater for growing grapes. The newly graduated Ibrahim tested out his knowledge in the square, while the delicate Emily found a smooth rock to sit on where she spent hours looking off into the distance. When she got home in the evening, she mentioned Mahmoudiya in her diary as part of a series of images inspired by her Protestant Old-Testament upbringing.

> *It is the most beautiful overlook to the Mediterranean. Here Noah planted his first vine that sprouted beneath the Lord's throne after the flood. Surely, with the sun's warmth it will produce plump grapes from which can be made the most miraculous wine. And why not, are we not but a few short miles from where Jesus performed his first miracle, in Cana of Galilee?*

Unlike his brother Younis, who longed for life's clamor and tumult, Ibrahim never left his parents' village house and would slip into Tel Safra on a daily basis from where he worked in Beirut at the Agronomia Company, which sold agricultural products and pesticides. Emily accompanied him back and forth every day for two years during which she taught Arabic at the International College Institute. But when she became pregnant with Zakariya, which was in the springtime, she could not imagine how she could possibly leave her child at home alone or in the care of anyone but herself, no matter who. So, she informed the school administration that she would not be returning to teach the following year. From that time on, the daughter of the director of the American University in Beirut Press imprisoned herself in the Mubarak family home until the end. Siblings coming from Damascus would go up to check on her once or twice a year, or an old maternal aunt who'd migrated from Palestine, and they would be baffled by her decision to live there among the villagers. Her pale complexion worried them, and Raheel caught their attention before they went back home, having lost the image of the educated young woman whose bright future her father had wagered so much on, up until the day she stopped being able to breathe. They took her to the hospital, and on the way, she instructed Marta who had accompanied her in the ambulance not to grieve for her, before giving up the spirit to a severe case of pneumonia.

She had spent a few years with her mother-in-law, who fate did not permit to rest very long from the oppression of her husband Jibrail as she quickly followed after him in death. She fell asleep and never woke up, leaving Emily behind with her two children and Raheel. Emily acknowledged in her diary that she felt closer to that sick woman than to sane people. She was able to communicate with her fully, to calm her down if she got angry. She'd take her by the hand out to the balcony to enjoy the fresh air. She kept her company, sang to her and spoke to her as if she had her full wits about her without expecting her to respond.

She kept pursuing the wine project with her husband, the project that had gotten stuck in the development stage for a long time due to Ibrahim's hesitance while she encouraged him to invest in Mahmoudiya. But no one told her that despite the passing of more than a century since the 1860 massacre, and two generations, if not three, since the return of victorious Philomena from the United States, that inheriting land in those parts also brought with it all animosities big and small. And so, it wasn't long before the thing that was expected to happen happened.

the truck and got out with his friend to face the two angry men who were annoyed by the thick cloud of dust. Ibrahim realized immediately that they were Druze locals, the ones who owned the adjoining land, Nassif and Mahmoud Hamdan.

"Couldn't you slow down a bit? The dust blinded us…"

"I wasn't going fast. You could have moved back a little."

That comment didn't sit well with Nassif, the one in the jacket.

"And in the first place, what gives you the right to pass this way?"

"I was going to my land!"

"And you drive through my land just like that? Without even a please or a thank you?"

Things got testy and the arak aided in raising the tone of the normally peaceful Ibrahim. Mahmoud Hamdan appeared to be more in solidarity with his cousin than Ibrahim's co-worker— the agricultural expert from the city, was with him, having found himself in the middle of a battle he tried in vain to defuse. But fists went up threateningly in faces, and the stream of insults gushed forth as Ibrahim surprised his co-worker with his determination in that quarrel, which spontaneously developed into shoves then blows and ended up with Ibrahim managing to throw Nassif to the ground. The latter got up with eyes burning with anger, pulled out the revolver he had concealed in his jacket and pointed it at Ibrahim. Rather than running away or taking cover, Ibrahim—the father of Zakariya Mubarak—swooped down on the man. When recalling the events of the fight as he told the story to his wife Emily, Ibrahim had no idea from where he had gotten the courage to grab his attacker's hand, without a thought, either to push the barrel of the gun away or to try to take it from him. They struggled, both of them grabbing for the gun. It went off. One bullet was fired. Everyone stopped in their tracks. Then came a cry of pain from Nassif who'd been hit in the leg. Suddenly the four men realized the gravity and absurdity of what they'd gotten themselves into.

Ibrahim sobered up. He took his foe who was bleeding profusely to the house of a local doctor who tried to stop the bleeding and disinfect the wound. Then some of Nassif's relatives came and took him to the hospital in Beirut. Meanwhile, Ibrahim went back home and decided after consulting with his wife and co-worker to go down to the police station and turn himself in. The judge ordered him to be remanded in custody in Raml Prison. He remained there for three months, persevering through the agony of living side by side with the lowliest of convicts, and all the annoying smells, and sleeping in rows shoulder-to-shoulder, all during the same time period when the doctors had no other choice but to amputate Nassif Hamdan's leg. But the judge gave Ibrahim a reduced sentence on the basis that the gun belonged to his adversary, and there had been two eyewitnesses whose corroborating statements indicated that it was Nassif who initiated the death threat. The judge ruled that Ibrahim had served sufficient time in jail and ordered him to pay compensation to the victim for the medical expenses needed to cover the cost of a prosthetic leg. His lawyer told him he could appeal that decision, but Ibrahim agreed to pay the fine for the sake of keeping the peace.

Nassif Hamdan and his family no longer had cause for revenge, but hearts were filled with hard feelings once again. Passing through to Mahmoudiya became even more difficult with the growing necessity to use a car for each trip. The narrow dirt mule path no longer served its purpose. For that reason, and also due to his lack of funds, Ibrahim gave up on the orchard and wine project once and for all. It appealed to him to recall with Emily the story of Astarte and the myth of the anemones. Meanwhile the Hamdans proceeded to fence in their land in order to avoid the establishment of a "de facto" road to Mahmoudiya Orchard, which the law might legitimize later.

Due to the continuous neglect of the orchard, the neighbors came to think of it as abandoned property, so a poor man, a father with a big family, got encouraged to farm the lower terraces, which he reached from below via Hajal Valley. He planted vegetables and put a lot of effort into watering and transporting them to the main road to Beirut, where he erected a small tent and displayed his cabbages, cucumbers, tomatoes, squash, and green beans. Passing cars would stop sometimes to buy from him. And in an unbelievably unfair turn of events, that poor man got chased down by the curse of Mahmoudiya Orchard when a truck coming from Syria lost its brakes and crashed into the tent and into him. His vegetables scattered everywhere, and he was thrown half dead over the cliff. By some miracle, his young son, who helped his father by carrying bags of vegetables out to the customers' cars, was unharmed.

People also talked about a woman who often roamed the fields in search of wild arugula and asparagus that she'd sell in bunches door-to-door. She happened to come upon a wild mushroom one time in Mahmoudiya, which she ate and ended up dying from after suffering unbearable intestinal pain. Or they talked about a conjured demon that overwhelmed two young men from the town while they were digging at the bottom of the southern slope in search of a buried treasure. They were panic-stricken and arrived in town out of breath.

The story of that orchard, which Philomena bought in the 1920s with gold from Michel Lagrange, the revolutionary who'd turned to exploiting the faith of naïve American evangelicals, didn't end there. After many years, it was woken up by a thirty-year-old lawyer and member of one of the Christian political parties, who used to visit the Mubarak family in Tel Safra and had given the neighbors the impression he was interested in Marta, who would scurry out of sight whenever she heard him coming to the door with a bouquet of roses in his hand.

Marta had a light complexion and took care of her figure. She walked for exercise and lacked some elegance in her clothing. She was stuck in Tel Safra where she found no young men around to open her heart to, and no one came asking for her hand either. Even the young men who lived in town year-round who'd quit school did not consider the daughter of that big house within their reach, and so life went on with that cloud of ambiguity hanging over her. As for the ones she conversed and mixed with, they were few in number. And each one had a "defect." The shock of her life was the young man who'd brought a list of everything he owned and all the money he had in the bank, and asked her to reciprocate with a list of her own worldly possessions. So, she shunned him and stopped answering his phone calls.

There was another young man who hadn't been after her personal properties but wanted her to go live with him in Beirut after Zakariya had left, and it was impossible for her to be so far from her mother and aunt. Lots of stories circulated about her romantic escapades, things she wished would have happened, but they were mere accusations, and she was innocent of all of them.

That lawyer was one of the ones Marta wished to befriend, but she couldn't find a way to do it. She listened to him as he spoke, how he expressed his dismay that the Mubarak family could accept being stripped of their right to pass to their land, something which was provided to them under the Real Estate Ownership Law of 1930.

On his next visit, he brought a booklet with him and read article 74 aloud.

"The owner of a property that is surrounded on all sides, and which does not have access to the public road, has the right to request a road easement through the adjacent land in return for payment of compensation proportional to any damages it might cause..."

It was an occasion for him to commend the French Mandate that had "left us the foundation of a nation of laws," as he put it, and to disparage independence and politicians. That lawyer was president of the Land Committee inside his political party, whose mission was to encourage Christians and help them hold onto their properties and refuse to sell them to other sects after an increase in transfers of ownership to Muslims had been recorded in the mixed areas. And along with some colleagues of his, he was working on drafting a law to prohibit the transfer of real estate properties between Christians and Muslims, except in special cases provided for by the law such as mixed marriages and the right of preemption and similar exemptions. But of course the idea remained a figment in the imaginations of its creators, because the law didn't hold up against the first objection.

Marta was impressed by the lawyer's eloquence, taken in by his hand gestures and the tone of his voice, because most of what he said went right over her head.

The important thing was that before Zakariya left, he signed a power of attorney with no expiration date authorizing the lawyer to pursue right of way to the property in his absence.

For Marta, it was her fate to be disappointed once again when she learned that the lawyer got engaged to another lawyer colleague of his he'd met only one month earlier in one of the courthouses, whose combination of eloquence and femininity had enchanted him. Marta put an end to those meetings with the lawyer to go over the case that he worked on persistently over the course of two decades during which gray strands began appearing on his head. That was also the time when everyone lived through the Israeli invasion of Lebanon and all the killings and forced relocations between Druze and Christians, which brought the work of the courts in those areas to a halt.

When relative stability was reestablished and the government gained back some semblance of a presence, the Hamdan family refused to resolve the dispute by mutual consent when the lawyer brought the matter to them in an effort to avoid incurring the expense of settling it in court. They didn't offer him coffee and didn't respond to his offer, either. One of them told him it was a waste of time and that the amount suggested was trivial, of no value. The lawyer took it to the courts and the stonewalling started with dodging receipt of the subpoena, which led to his having to reissue the subpoena within the legally allotted time limits, eventually requiring him to post it on the door of the courthouse pursuant to due process. That was followed by failures to appear in court, an attempt to gain time and delay the appointment of a lawyer, and the presentation of medical excuses. After that came a slew of objections, starting with doubting the expert appointed to delineate the road easement under the pretext that he was a Christian and might be biased toward the opposing side. So that expert was replaced with another expert from the Shiite sect whom they refused to accompany when he visited the site, only to object on the basis that the road he suggested for access to Mahmoudiya would cause major damages to the land it passed through and to its owners, and then suggest another long road going straight uphill from the lowest point of Hajal Valley.

Added to all that was a whole lot of bickering, a refusal to take compensation in Lebanese liras after its value plummeted with respect to the U.S. dollar, threats to appeal to warlords for help, and the issuing of sharp public statements such as, "We are not to be overlooked," and "Our flesh is too tough to chew." It got to where the judge was nearing age sixty-seven and was certain not to conclude the case before reaching retirement age, so he handed it over to a new colleague who asked for an extension so he could familiarize himself with the facts of the case and issue subpoenas, which resulted in the lodging of appeals. Finally, after eighteen years, a ruling was issued whereby the owners of Mahmoudiya could take possession of and pave the road easement leading to their land. It specified the required fee to be paid in return and that it should be deposited in the court registry in case the opposing side refused receipt. However, the Hamdan family's lawyer lodged an appeal, so a further investigation into the case took more than two additional years, at the end of which the judge confirmed the original ruling.

The Druze legal team was headed by Akram Bin Nassif Hamdan who claimed that doctors confirmed to him that his father died of the bullet wound to his leg even though there had been a seven-year gap between the fight and his death, and that the road easement had been paid for in blood and wasn't going to pass just like that. He kept repeating the phrase, "Tomorrow is just a day away," which he wanted to be taken as a threat: "Whoever wants to open a road on our land, let him come find us in Tel Safra…"

The lawyer did not try to carry out the ruling but rather relayed the information to Marta. He came knocking at the door without an appointment so she couldn't dodge him and handed her the documents as he stood there at the door. She didn't invite him in and asked him to wait while she brought an envelope containing the remaining balance of what they owed him for his troubles. He tried to refuse, saying that he worked on such cases out of his duty as a Christian, but she insisted, in order to prove that she was done with him, still convinced that he had deceived her in spite of no promises ever having been made between them or even any kind of romantic confessions from either of them during a relationship that had been limited to a few simple touches and smiles.

And so, age crept up on Marta Mubarak, and rather than easing up on her conditions for marriage, she tightened them. She clung to her life as a single woman, without a man, and grew accustomed to the life of women with her mother and her aunt, after Zakariya left.

When Marta received the judge's ruling on the right-of-way to Mahmoudiya Orchard, she didn't do anything. What means did she have, with no one in her corner besides her sick mother, to pave a road, especially when it involved breaking down the property fence and uprooting the trees that stood in the way, delineating its borders, paving it with gravel and then paving it with asphalt so cars could pass, and at a time when the orchard was still in a state of neglect.

She kept the maps and waited for Zakariya's return. He looked them over quickly a few days after arriving and then folded them up and decided to postpone looking into the matter until after dealing with the *Blue Violinist* painting and carrying out what he'd planned to do after he returned.

But Marta kept pushing him to pursue his rights or else those rights would die with the passage of time. The lawyer had deposited the requested sum they had to pay for the road at the court registry, and it was not their fault if the other side didn't collect it. During that summer of his return to Tel Safra, Zakariya headed to Mahmoudiya Orchard just one time. He brought the map with him and tried to see where the road was that the judge had delineated for them. He stood for a long time next to the fence that surrounded the Hamdans' property when Nassif's son showed up, having been told by one of his relatives that Zakariya was in the neighborhood. It was unknown exactly what transpired between them, but they were seen having a discussion and waving their hands around before Zakariya went back home saying that the orchard was inhabited by a devil. After Zakariya's death, Marta remembered how he had looked at her for a long time that day and advised her to sell Mahmoudiya the first chance she got. Then he stopped as if an idea had just popped into his head.

"Why don't you give it to our cousins, Uncle Younis's sons, and put an end to our dispute with them? We've borne responsibility for that land for an entire century!"

"*I* should sell it?" she asked, looking at him with surprise. "Give it to *my* cousins? Why are you telling me to do such things? Where are you going?"

He didn't answer and stayed lost in thought for a moment before snapping out of it and insisting that he would never back down from the Hamdans, no matter the cost. He suddenly appeared stern and ready for the worst. His sister had never seen him that way. It was as if he wanted a confrontation and wanted to cross the point of no return, up until he was found shot in the pine grove, on the hill overlooking Mahmoudiya

Orchard, as though sitting there, gazing from the distance upon the land of his great-grandmother—Philomena, daughter of Bahiya Murad.

14

From the very beginning, the security officials never stopped imagining the worst; that is, that some Druze men had been involved in the murder of Zakariya Mubarak, the Christian, in Tel Safra. Right after the crime was reported, and despite accusations automatically pointing to the victim's relatives, a big van was sent to the town's police station with ten police officers on board, which caused problems at the station where they had difficulty finding sleeping quarters for all of them. Leading the way and clearing the path for the van was a Jeep with a carefully chosen lieutenant riding in the passenger seat up front. He had been briefed on the special character of that mixed town, which had been able to overcome the "painful" events that had taken place there before the lieutenant was born without resorting to clashes or forced displacements as had been the case in most mixed villages. But after Younis Mubarak's sons showed up at their cousin's funeral and the idea circulated that under the law, killing Zakariya would not bring the cousins any share of the family inheritance, the townspeople immediately fell back on another possibility. They could not leave the crime as something ambiguous looming over them. So, an idea bubbled to the surface in whispers, within a tight circle whose members stopped themselves from saying too much for fear of fanning a fire that might get out of control—the idea that the Druze Hamdans were trying to even an old score with the Maronite Mubaraks. The parallel suddenly seemed enticing: a bullet for a bullet, despite half a century between them. The first from the father of Zakariya Mubarak to the leg of the father of Nassif Hamdan and today, a return shot from Nassif to Zakariya's chest, and both events occurring in two locations that were no more than five hundred meters apart.

In her turn, Marta, who was still claiming her relatives were to blame, woke up one morning to add the Hamdans to the list of suspects. Her aunt Raheel had gotten the gist of what she said and repeated it arbitrarily in earshot of the assistant investigating judge.

Kamal Abu Khalid had been avoiding going back to the house in Tel Safra and listening to Marta. He felt she was deliberately misleading him, but he wasn't going to be able to overlook any detail. He was still mired in the possibilities related to the Chagall painting. He'd been interrogating the young man who had accompanied Badih Makhlouf to the Mubaraks' house and was investigating here and there into friends of the Albino. He called on one of his assistants to subpoena all the male owners of the properties adjacent to the orchard, of whom there were four—Nassif Hamdan's two sons and their two paternal cousins—in order to question them separately and verify their whereabouts that day.

The series of interrogations made one fact very clear: long-term memory was alive and well in Tel Safra. The investigators listened to a long and rambling story that the Hamdan family circulated about the fight between their father and Zakariya's father over the easement to the orchard: True, their father had pulled out his weapon, but he'd only done it to scare Ibrahim Mubarak and his companion, not with intent to kill, and Zakariya's father had been hiding a gun of his own in his belt, and that was the gun that went off and shot Nassif Hamdan in the leg, causing his eventual death. And one of them added without being asked that if they'd wanted to take revenge for their father, then they would have done so in plain sight, supporting his position with the adage, "Vengeance doesn't have to be 'tit for tat.'" They forfeited their right to that before the court, and they were not going to go back on their decision because they were people of their word. And one of them delved into the past, to a previous century, and dug up the story of Mahmoudiya Orchard, claiming as though he were a specialist in modern Lebanese history that the Christians benefited at that time from the military support that European nations had afforded to them after the military campaign of Napoleon III on Lebanon in opposition to Ottoman rule—the "Sick Man" campaign. They benefited in the form of seizing Druze lands at rock-bottom prices, aided by the leader of the campaign, a man by the name of De Beaufort d'Hautpoul. Mahmoudiya Orchard was ceded to the Mubaraks by means of a trick, because Sheikh Salman Abi Nakad, who sold it to them, was not of sound mind, but they had waited until his mother died to send him a shrewd real estate agent who cheated him; he low-balled him on the price. They repeated what they all knew, that immediately upon the transfer of their property to the Mubaraks, the Mubaraks erected a huge cross at its border, which was proof of their hostile intentions.

159

In sum, what the investigating judge's assistants reported to him was that there was a lot of bitterness brewing in the hearts around there, and the four Hamdan sons gave proof that they had all been attending a big election rally in the city of Aley on that Sunday afternoon when Zakariya was murdered. One of them—the one who had confidently traced everything back to historical events—had even recited a fiery poem right there on the stage. They pulled up pictures on their cell phones to prove it to the investigator. Nothing was recorded in the interrogation transcript except the testimony of the one called Akram Nassif Hamdan who told the investigator that he had encountered Zakariya Mubarak a few weeks prior to his murder. Zakariya had been holding a map in his hand that he said delineated a legal easement to Mahmoudiya through the Hamdans' property. Most of the conversation had been exchanged calmly, and Akram informed Zakariya that the matter could not be solved by a court ruling. The discussion got a bit heated between them but, in the end, they shook hands before going back to their homes.

Amid all that confusion, and ten full days after the crime had been committed, a development came about that no one saw coming. A young man came into the Palace of Justice in Baabda during official working hours. He wore a ponytail and was carrying a backpack on his shoulders that caught one's attention because he didn't look like the kind of person who usually came to that dignified place. He asked to see the investigating judge in charge of the Tel Safra case. He entered and introduced himself, and also told him about the Ancient Paths Club. He told Kamal Abu Khalid how he and his friends had discovered the body the Sunday before last, before the police arrived on the

160

scene. This was a big surprise because the young man's name and the name of their club had not appeared in any reports that had come into the investigating judge's hands.

"Would you agree to give your statement now, since in any case I'll be calling you in as a witness?"

The transcriber came in and the student gave his testimony.

"We congregated not far from the victim, but the police, when they arrived, shooed us away, so we continued on our way."

"Without taking your statements?!"

The investigating judge already started preparing in his mind what he would say to the Tel Safra police chief. Little did he know, the scandal was just beginning.

"I'm a student in the College of Medicine at Saint Joseph University, and I'm the one who ascertained the man was dead before anyone arrived."

The judge crossed his arms and looked up, not knowing who to appeal to for help.

"Can you estimate what time the crime occurred?"

"He didn't appear rigid to me, so he hadn't been dead very long, an hour at most, so between 4:00 and 4:30."

"Is that everything?"

"No. I asked to see you today in order to tell you that while I was bending down to check the victim for a heartbeat, I saw a gun nearby shining in the brush. And I'm certain it was a Glock 17, the latest model."

"And how do you know it was a Glock 17?" Abu Khalid interrupted.

"I recognized it from seeing them in the hands of the detectives on CSI: LA. I'm addicted to that series."

"How far would you estimate the distance was between where the victim's right hand was and where the gun was tossed?"

The student hesitated and then confirmed that the gun had been far away from the body, around three meters, and that its distance had caught his attention right from the start.

"And you come in to tell me about all this after ten days? Are you aware that I can charge you with withholding evidence?"

"I understand, but I assumed the two policemen found the gun."

A nervous smile appeared on Kamal Abu Khalid's face as he shook his head menacingly. "Did you see any people or cars in the area?"

"No. All we heard after a little while on our way down to Hajal Valley were sirens from ambulances speeding toward the place."

The judge asked him for a list of the names of his colleagues in the Ancient Paths Club, and their addresses and phone numbers. He let him go on his own recognizance and immediately went to call the police chief to seek permission to open an investigation into the officers at the Tel Safra precinct on charges of egregious procedural errors.

He began by questioning the subordinate, the driver of the Jeep, who verified that the sergeant did indeed let the hikers go without heeding his advice to take their statements before they left, and he insisted that he did not see any weapon at the crime scene. The investigator made it clear to him that he was risking his job if he withheld any information, as it would amount to impeding the investigation. The man did not hold up long to the jail threats and confessed that on the next day and amid the commotion caused by the arrival of additional officers to the police station, he slept near the sergeant in a shared room and noticed him trying to hide a gun in the drawer—not his police-issue American model. It was a new weapon, and the jeep driver didn't recognize the model.

After that, the judge asked for the sergeant to be brought in for questioning. The sergeant tried at first to appear cooperative by handing over the cartridge that he had gone back to look for at the crime scene. Kamal Abu Khalid placed it in an envelope and sent it to the ballistics lab before beginning the interrogation.

"How did you find out about the crime?"

"Someone called it into the station on a landline, so we weren't able to trace the number of the caller, and he refused to identify himself."

"And you refused to note that in your report, naturally, since documenting evidence at the Tel Safra station is discretionary!"

After the sarcasm Kamal Abu Khalid got serious and went to the heart of the matter. "Where's the Glock 17?"

As was his habit, the investigator liked to strike while the iron was hot. The sergeant tried to buy some time.

"What's that? Some kind of cell phone?"

The judge warned him not to play games and told him there was a witness who had seen him pick up the gun when it was discovered near the victim and tuck it into his pocket. The sergeant stammered and then decided to cut his losses. He softened his tone and started complaining about his destitute circumstances and began listing the cost of rent and medicine, before Abu Khalid interrupted him.

"But you are covering up the crime of first-degree murder and covering for the perpetrator of that crime!"

The sergeant went back to his theory.

"The criminal is known, Sir. It was his cousins. They killed him over a disagreement over the inheritance."

The investigator rebuked him saying it was *his* responsibility to find the perpetrator and it was the police's job to preserve evidence, not conceal it and insist on misleading the investigation.

"That is a crime!"

He realized he was screaming and so he got himself back under control.

"Where's the gun?"

The sergeant broke down.

"I sold it."

The judge blew up again, pounded the desk with his hand.

"Are you crazy?"

On his day off, the sergeant had given it to one of his relatives, who was supposed to sell it and then bring him the money. He was still waiting for the money.

The sergeant's nephew was brought in. He was a young man who was easy to deal with. He brought the money in as soon as he was summoned. He could see that his uncle the military man was defeated, so he confessed, telling the investigator about a friend of his who'd found an M16 rifle with four clips and two boxes of ammunition leftover from the civil war in his parents' house after the friend's father passed away. So the friend sold them. That friend was the one who led him to the dealer who'd bought the rifle and ammunition from him. It became clear from the quick series of follow-up interrogations conducted by the Department of National Security that the Glock 17 had circulated around Beirut until a well-known arms dealer ended up offering it to its original owner, Badih Makhlouf, saying, "Take this one. It's just the kind you like—an expensive one you can sell to the well-to-do!"

The investigator brought Badih Makhlouf back in for questioning. Makhlouf told the investigator that after he'd been questioned the first time, someone offered to sell him the gun at a decent price. He recognized the gun and bought it—the same gun he'd given to Zakariya Mubarak as a gift. He said he was in the process of getting in touch with the investigator when he got the summons, so he'd brought the Glock 17 with him to leave at the disposal of the investigation. And he reminded Kamal Abu Khalid how cooperative he was being with the police.

The investigator sent the gun, along with the bullet and the empty cartridge, to the scientific laboratory of the General Directorate of Internal Security while he waited for the report, and issued a warrant for the arrest of the Tel Safra chief of police on charges of tampering with a crime scene, embezzling a murder weapon, and obstructing an investigation. And he demanded his immediate incarceration.

The interview with the young ambulance driver and the young redheaded volunteer who accompanied him did not add any new details to the sequence of events. They confirmed that they had taken the body to the town hospital only after getting permission from the sergeant and the medical examiner first. But before leaving the interview the young woman said that she had reminded them both at the time that they should call in the forensics team, but they didn't see any need for that.

The dialogue with the medical examiner was strange.

"I arrived at the crime scene in the dark and I have poor vision…"

"And that hair of yours," the inspector interrupted sarcastically, "is it fake?"

The medical examiner, who was still congested, smiled, and blew his nose as he straightened his toupee.

"Your report doesn't say anything: 'The bullet entered along the windpipe and penetrated the heart on the side of the spinal column.' You didn't indicate whether the bullet had been fired from bottom to top or vice versa. Could you determine if the bullet had been fired at the victim from a distance or close up?

Do I have to teach you your profession all over again?"

"I tried to check for any evidence of gunpowder, which might prove it had been shot at close range. But it was too dark and also the ambulance medic's flashlight died. She was shining it on the area for me."

"So, what did you all do?"

"We tried to use the car headlights, to no avail."

The judge let out a nervous laugh.

"*La hawla wa la quwwa illa bil-Lah*! Only God can help us! You moved the victim to the hospital, where they removed his clothing and washed him. Does this kind of chaos happen with you people every time?"

"We rarely need to do investigations, since in the vast majority of cases the assailants are known. It was said that this man's killers were known by name."

"And when was this 'said'?"

"As soon as the body arrived at the hospital…"

He would postpone recommending that they stop seeking that medical examiner's services, but he wasn't going to let him go unpunished for such extreme negligence.

Similar accounts came in the course of the testimony given by the members of the Ancient Paths Club who were questioned individually about what they saw. Some of them said it was the first time they had ever seen a dead body up close and noted that his color was a frightening shade of white. Some felt that the sergeant had been in a hurry to get rid of them, that he'd kicked them out, and none of them had seen a gun lying in the grass. The last of the interviews was with a young woman who stuck around a bit longer than her colleagues in the judge's office, and as she was leaving, she praised Kamal Abu Khalid's character. He detained her to pose some additional questions after she surprised him by saying out loud what had started to take shape in his mind after the discovery of the gun, about the dead man's facial features having a look of profound anguish. She believed that he had chosen that beautiful view and that splendid autumn weather to put an end to his life.

He asked her again, "You think the man committed suicide?"

"Yes."

"And how can you be so sure?"

"It was the feeling I got the moment I saw him."

She shrugged her shoulders as she answered, as if what she was saying was not important to anyone other than herself in any case, and so the investigating judge said to himself, *"And why not?"*

And an observation made by one of Kamal Abu Khalid's assistants also attested to the same idea. "We found the murder weapon near the victim, and all the suspects and everyone who had something to gain from Zakariya Mubarak's death all have firm alibis and witnesses, with the exception of the victim himself."

The joke did not sit well with the investigating judge who saw himself in this case as being like a circus performer letting go of one rope hanging in the air only to grab onto another, even though he felt with the testimony of the members of the Ancient Paths Club that this time the rope he'd grabbed hold of was secure.

15

Zakariya booked a one-way plane ticket. He didn't take any of his clothes or shoes to Boston. He slung the cylinder with *The Blue Violinist* over his shoulder, and in his carry-on he packed his ten Arabic books and two hats—the summer one and the winter one. In his jacket pockets he put his passport, his mother's diary, and the certificate of authenticity signed by Marc Chagall. All in addition, of course, to his new cargo, Jane Malloy, who napped for hours during the flight behind a black sleep mask.

He didn't sleep a wink. He kept watch over her; even when his arm went numb, he didn't pull it out from behind her head, to avoid waking her. And so, there on the Boeing 747, they divided up their roles. She went forth in her life knowing he was behind her whichever way she turned. In a matter of days, Zakariya Mubarak of Tel Safra and product of southern Mount Lebanon, was enchanted by this young woman of Irish descent whose grandparents had immigrated to the United States in the 1940s to escape the great famine that plagued their island.

She gulped bourbon in big swigs like a man, never stopped receiving and answering messages on her cell phone, swore profusely left and right, and described herself as the rotted branch, since families in her view got sick like trees. The halo that Zakariya wrapped around her expanded to include her father, who lived alone in the suburb of Somerville, looked after by a home caregiver from El Salvador who came for an hour every morning. He was an enigmatic man, blue eyes, a sculpted face tilled with wrinkles. She introduced him to her friend, "Zach, from Lebanon."

With that abbreviated version of his name that rolled off her tongue, she baptized him as an American. Her father didn't utter a word, as if he hadn't heard what she said. He sat there on a rocking chair out on the porch, didn't get up to greet them, and likewise didn't get up to see them out. He gave Zakariya the impression that he was just biding his time until his only child and her boyfriend left so he could go back to staring into the deep chasm inside himself. But then suddenly, after they had given up all hope of hearing his voice, he spoke. He asked Jane if her friend was Jewish, to which she disdainfully answered that she didn't know, and didn't want to know. Zakariya answered that he was an Arab, so her father thought he was Muslim. "No, I'm Christian." It appeared difficult for Mr. Malloy to reconcile that, and so, tired by the short conversation, he sank back into his utter silence. His house was elegant, surrounded by bare poplar trees that a friendly squirrel was climbing on, and winter jasmine and camellia flowers.

When they went out to the wide street, Jane told him as she brushed off a tear with the back of her hand that her father had spent his life in a steel factory, twenty years of which were spent over a welding machine that ruined his eyes. When he retired, her mother realized that she would be with him face-to-face all day long, so she left the house after an argument one night and nothing was heard from her again, and no one went looking for her, either. Her clothes and pictures from her teen years were all still at the house. Jane was afraid she might find her back at home one day and wouldn't know what to do. She loved her parents a lot, loved both of them, each in a different way, but she couldn't stand living with the two of them together. A single day would be guaranteed to relaunch the shouting matches and cause them to separate all over again.

Jane, too, was not going to live in Boston. She wanted a place of her own, someplace new that wasn't burdened with memories. During the week that she and Zakariya spent in the city, Jane was anxious and talked a long time on the phone. She'd step away from Zakariya to talk freely and then come back having made up her mind. At the first used car dealership she went to, she bought the red GMC Sierra with four-wheel-drive that was parked out front on display. She paid for it with a credit card and told Zakariya to wait for her at a coffee shop that was bustling with students. She was a skilled driver. She blew him a kiss from her hand. She was gone for hours, came back in the afternoon, and then they headed west. They would travel the continent from coast to coast. She said she had "an important appointment" in Seattle, a three-thousand-mile drive from Boston.

They took turns behind the wheel. Zakariya tipped his hat down over his forehead and Jane put on dark sunglasses. He'd drive and she would sleep. She'd drive and he would gaze at her while she sang along loudly with the songs playing on the radio. At the motels, they would make love as soon as they woke up. After that, he'd bring her coffee and glazed donuts. He had his fill of roadside restaurants and promised Jane all the flavors of the East if they settled down in a house together. "You will discover Zakariya the great chef." She didn't answer. She wasn't ready and hadn't been born for keeping house. She read John Fante and Norman Mailer, and couldn't stand spending evening hours in the house. Zakariya would wake up around midnight and not find her at home. He'd run out into the street, go into the closest nightclub that was still open, and find her sitting at the bar between two men, exchanging funny toasts and jokes with them, as if they were old friends of hers. He'd take her back to the hotel, stammering, having started with beer and ended with whiskey, barely able to stay on her feet.

In Chicago, she bought cigarette rolling papers near a gas station, and after that Zakariya could smell marijuana on her clothes whenever he hugged her to his chest. At a fast-food restaurant in North Dakota, she asked him for the first time what he had inside that metal tube of his that he never parted with, even when he went to the bathroom. He told her his French saga, exaggerating his romantic escapades, and even ventured into Mathilde Lagrange's illness, but he steered clear of the story of *The Blue Violinist*. She mocked him for womanizing with an old lady and said that if she fell in love with him and he left her, she'd stab him in the heart. He told her about Tel Safra and about his grandfather Jibrail, how he used to carry him on his shoulders and parade him around on Palm Sunday. He continued that tradition until Zakariya turned ten, which is when his grandfather started advising him about the "fruit of this world." Women, in other words. He avoided asking her about her past. He was jealous of her and the things she did without him before they met in the Black Forest. It seemed to him from little details and proper nouns that her life hadn't been a lake of calm waters.

172

They spent more than forty days on the road. He realized that his love for Jane Malloy was not waning. He couldn't get his fill of gazing at her, to the point that she would wake up in the morning and scold him. "I don't want you to look at me while I'm sleeping."

He'd smile and wish they would stay together forever, all alone in that little motel—the Three Roses, run by that sixty-year-old woman, Mrs. Jay-Parker, who named it that after her three daughters who took off with random passersby, leaving her all alone, surrounded by Siamese cats and tropical plants in clay pots, in a remote stretch far from the highway. There he secretly disconnected the battery cable one night, causing Jane to find a dead motor the next morning when she tried to start the car. Jane got mad. She started pounding on the hood with both hands as if some disaster had struck. Stopping put her face-to-face with herself, as she said, face-to-face with her unbearable hardships. The only life for her was to keep going.

"I'm a woman wanderer. If I settle down, I'll die."

He'd stroke her gently, pick her up in his arms and carry her, whispering to her that his grandmother had come to America and returned carrying English gold pounds, and now he was going to go back to his homeland carrying Jane Malloy. Her face would light up and she'd surrender to an unreachable daydream.

They made it to Seattle.

Jane took off in the car and disappeared for an entire day, a day during which he was lost without her. He remembered his family at home, so he bought a cell phone near the hotel and tried to call Tel Safra. He didn't get through. He stayed up all night. He took out his mother's diary while waiting for Jane and opened it to a random page.

Saturday, July 25

Nothing outside beckons to me, nothing in Beirut, no one in this beautiful town. I don't dare sit in the shade of the leafy walnut tree in front of the house. I have no energy to chitchat with the neighbors or other passersby. Marta and Zakariya love people. I envy them for that…

Jane returned in the morning and fell asleep in his lap, as she did every night. At noon she said they still had enough money to continue their trip. He didn't comment. Her secrets were piling up.

They headed east on the captain's orders. To New York again, to the other coast. His grandmother had come to that city by sea from the east, and now here he was coming to it by land from the west. But he started getting tired. His mood had changed. He felt Jane was towing him along and that the nomadic Bedouin life wasn't for him.

She did it again on the road, in the car. It came time for her to take the wheel after passing through Minneapolis.

"You didn't tell me what you've got there on your shoulder? Do you want me to steal it while you're sleeping?"

"It's a despicable story. Doesn't make me look good."

"Tell it to me anyway. Maybe I'll score a few points on you."

"On condition you tell me what you're hiding from me in Boston and Seattle, even though I sometimes think I prefer being enveloped in your secrets…"

She laughed out loud.

"This world has not changed one bit. The easterner is still inventing a girl out of his own imagination!"

He didn't hide anything from her. He tried to describe that night in Saint-Paul-de-Vence when he wavered between his loyalty and affection for the owner of The Sunflower and the innate urge to run away that was inside him, which made him pick up the painting that night and take off with it.

"And how will you sell it?"

"I don't know!"

"You're a thief. You're an outlaw!"

She was happy about his predicament. It made them equal, because when her turn came around, her confession was a big surprise. She had a school friend in Boston who composed the music for a lot of songs that never made the pop charts, so he started working as a mid-level drug dealer out of the back room of the recording studio. He'd hidden ten kilos of cocaine in the motor of the GMC and sent it with Jane to Seattle, where she delivered it to the man's associates at a vehicle graveyard near the port. It seemed the long distance was guaranteed to throw the Office of Drug Control off their trail. She got her commission.

"I actually provide for the 'home' while you carry an imaginary fortune on your shoulder…"

He appeared distressed, so she tried to cheer him up.

"We're Bonnie and Clyde, but with no one on our trail!"

"And this need of yours to keep moving. 'If I settle down, I'll die.' That was all fake? You were making fun of me?"

She didn't answer. But after a little while, she pounded her hand on the steering wheel and screamed, "These are my big secrets. Are you happy now?"

At the one hundred twentieth meridian, they lost their virginity together in a matter of minutes, but they kept on driving in shifts while a long silence settled in between them that was intermittently interrupted by lukewarm comments about needing to stop for lunch or to fill up the gas tank. He would discover later that Jane had a criminal record; she'd been in juvenile detention for narcotics trafficking in high school before she'd turned eighteen. And also, later on her lawyer had succeeded in getting her off from another charge of association with a burglary ring.

For the first time, and without any prior planning, Zakariya fell asleep on his left shoulder while Jane fell asleep on her right, and most likely their dreams that night did not cross paths.

The next morning, Jane was driving when Marta Mubarak picked up the phone on the other side of the world. She burst out crying upon hearing her brother's voice. Zakariya asked Jane to pull over to the side of the highway, because it was an important matter.

"Mother is dead. We buried her two weeks ago, but I had no way to reach you. Emily is gone and I'm left here. Just me and Aunt Raheel."

His eyes welled up and he didn't know what to say, so Marta finished telling him how during the fits of coughing that gripped their mother during her final days, she urged her not to tell her brother about her failing health, in order not to ruin his life where he was, for "every soul has to taste death," she said.

Jane could not find the words to console him, so she kissed him on his eyes. At the next stop, Zakariya asked for two separate rooms. He didn't want Jane to have to bear his grief. He locked the door, threw himself face down onto the bed, and started sobbing. From time to time, he would pound the bed with his fist. He didn't eat anything for two days. Jane knocked at the door repeatedly and called to him, but he wouldn't come out no matter how much she pleaded with him. She left the pepperoni pizza and soft drink outside the door. "Food's out here."

"Don't worry about me. I just need to be alone one more day."

He opened Emily's diary again, read it aloud, sobbing.

> *My father taught me the love of letters. He was the director of the American University Press. The Arabic language was his second homeland, but he did not give me the key to the loathsome game of life. I always keep the copy of the Holy Quran that he gave me, and I think that over time I have memorized it. No, but I am able to complete any verse if I hear the opening line recited…*

After weeping, he realized there was no way around returning to his homeland. The clock had struck, and he had things there that were more stable. He would take his time planning his departure without telling Jane. He called Marta back and told her he would be returning to Tel Safra soon, but she didn't welcome the idea. Actually, she asked him to hold off on his decision. Life had taken him full circle. He'd come back to find himself in the same position as with every woman that had ever occupied his heart: looking for the right opportunity to escape.

When they got back on the road and continued on their way to New York, Zakariya got behind the wheel and gradually stepped harder and harder on the accelerator until the GMC's motor started rumbling for help, as if it had reached the end of its limits. At the same time, he turned the music up as high as it would go. Jane got scared. She held on tight to her seat and put her feet firmly on the floor of the car. The first thing that came to her mind was that Zakariya, who'd been shocked by the news of his mother's death, was flirting with danger and death.

She yelled at him to slow down and let her drive because the police were going to stop them for sure if they caught him on their radar, and he didn't have an American driver's license. At that speed, he might wind up in jail and get himself deported from the United States. He pretended he couldn't hear what she was saying over the sound of the motor, but he liked the idea of being deported and asked her sarcastically if she would join him too on a "work trip" toward the east coast of the United States, even if she was hiding cocaine inside the motor. She turned the radio down, so he turned it back up before suddenly deciding to stop on the side of the road. He got out nervously and opened the hood. He started searching for the bag of drugs inside the motor while she sat inside the car smoking and after a little while broke into tears. He slammed the hood shut and came closer to her. When he leaned over her, she slapped him on the cheek and screamed, "I do that for us, you idiot!"

"You were doing it before there was an 'us,' you liar!"

They fought each other violently. She wrapped her arm around his neck. He picked her up and flipped her over. She bit him on the wrist. He gave her a hard slap on her butt with his other hand. They exchanged all sorts of curses, some of which Zakariya said in Arabic. He emptied out his sadness over Emily's death and she emptied out her frustrations. Then they held each other in a long embrace. He leaned his back against the car door on the side next to the road and hugged her in his arms while the cars and trucks sped by them. One driver sounded his naval alarm horn celebrating the two infatuated lovers.

He clung to her all over again. He let her take the wheel when the sun behind them was starting to set and the road before them shimmered with a glistening mirage in the distance.

They were calm after having come through a violent battle, while an old hit blared on the radio.

"*I've been through the desert on a horse with no name. It felt good to be out of the rain…*"

16

They never entered New York. Jane stopped at a drugstore claiming she needed something for a headache. She was inside for a long time before coming back out to say that the elderly Jamaican pharmacy clerk was a chatterbox who didn't know how to end a story, especially since there weren't any other customers in there. When she got back in the car Zakariya sensed a new glint of enthusiasm in her eyes, about some crisis she was hiding from him, and her headache had magically gone away. She pestered him like a child to take the highway north, so he did. Her itineraries hid all sorts of surprises and the promise of danger, but the end was drawing near. She sensed something too, from small details, from a hand that no longer caressed her hand at every touch, from gazes that fell upon her less and less and got lost instead in the scenery. She sensed that Zakariya had started to break away from her.

"Don't worry. The car is 'clean.' We'll go see Niagara Falls and after that you can do whatever you want with your life. You don't have to run away from me. Just tell me when you get run-away fever so we can say goodbye to each other like mature adults."

They found a small room at Victoria Inn. Each one grabbed a cup of coffee the next morning and headed toward the roar of the flowing waters. She held his hand at the front ledge where the magnificent view freezes onlookers in their place, and they are unable to hear each other if they talk. As they stood there, entranced, at a surprise moment that she most definitely planned for from the beginning, ever since they'd left the route to New York and headed for the Canadian borders, Jane Malloy climbed nimbly onto the "Crazies' safety railing" and stood there on the second-to-last horizontal iron bar. She braced her knees against the top bar of the safety railing with the largest portion of her body suspended in the air, ready to fall at the slightest slip or if her weight tipped outward. That was what was happening right before Zakariya's eyes as he shouted to her. He climbed up behind her and wrapped his arms around her waist.

At least one person every week throws themself into those gushing waters; it is one of the most enticing places for those wishing to put an end to their lives—the hopeless, the bankrupt, and the depressed especially. The number of people who'd committed suicide there or risked trying to stand on the rocks and slipped and fell to their deaths was over five thousand. A small number fell onto the water falls and were saved, and afterward sank their teeth into life and bit down hard. Most of the victims were white men, while the number of women surpassed the number of Blacks. There's a lot of talk surrounding the allure of those waters. The tourist who lets themself get close to those turbulent waters without protection might fall under the spell of the precipice even if they hadn't been despairing of life or feeling brokenhearted.

Zakariya was screaming for help from the crowd that had gathered at the stone bench while he held onto her and prevented her from flying to the bottom, which is what it seemed she was about to do with her arms flailing in the air. She'd gone back to playing with danger the moment she felt a force holding her in place. She was lightweight, easy for him to pull back. But in the midst of all the commotion, the crowd of tourists, and some mostly Japanese young men and women who rushed to her aid, the idea of abandoning her popped into Zakariya's head. He could unwrap his arms from around her waist and let her fall into the distant depths, finish with the burden of her, find rest, and renew his life. That fleeting idea caused him to relax his grip for one second, or even less. Feeling that she had gone into the void, with no support, and that she was on her way down into the pit, Jane let out a sharp scream that emerged from deep inside her. Right then, Zakariya tightened his arms around her again subconsciously as numerous other hands reached out to Jane to bring her down from the railing.

She was laughing excitedly as she wiped the mist from her face. Once they could hear each other, she told him she was trying to test herself and test him.

"How so?"

"I gave you the chance to get rid of me and you didn't take it. Maybe you'll regret it later."

"You could have jumped. Why didn't you?"

"Not out of love for you. For your baby."

He didn't understand.

"I'm pregnant, just as I promised you in France in front of Strasbourg Cathedral."

He got so emotional his ears turned red.

"I don't believe it!"

"Think what you will, but I did a pregnancy test when I stopped at the drug store a few days ago on the route to New York, if you remember!"

The world turned upside down. A meteor had suddenly landed between them. He wasn't going anywhere. He wouldn't be seeing Tel Safra anytime soon. He'd entered in now, like in a dream he sometimes had, going the wrong way down a highway with no apparent way to turn back in the right direction.

———

She spent the first three months between morning sickness and daytime vomiting, in addition to constant fatigue, having to pee all the time, and mood swings. Jane did not need to be pregnant to switch in an instant from being content with very little to being angry for no reason.

Settling down had become a necessity, so they rented a house in Saratoga Springs with what was left of Jane's money. And Zakariya was able to find a job at a restaurant frequented at noon by office employees in the city center—The White Elephant. They tested him out for a week; they put him in charge of making the daily special: Fish *Siyadiyeh* with rice, onions, and saffron one time and Stuffed Eggplant *Sheikh el-Mahshi* another time, earning him the approval of the customers who asked for more of these strange and delicious eastern flavors. They insisted on meeting the chef personally, so Zakariya asked the owner of the restaurant to sponsor his work visa so he could then use it as a step toward permanent residency.

After his legal status was settled, they got married without any fanfare—him in his white shirt that had become his permanent attire, and her in her jeans showing the beginnings of her swelling belly, with two administration workers from the mayor's office standing as witnesses. They followed it up with an evening get-together for the two of them out on the porch; it was then that Zakariya smoked some marijuana with Jane for the first time. He discovered that she had been growing it behind his back in pots that she would move around to keep them in the sun as much as possible. They looked like the flowerpots that his sister Marta spread around the house in Tel Safra. And they drank a whole bottle of cheap French champagne, just the two of them, all so their child would have two legitimate parents.

At the restaurant, and in spite of how much he loved feeding others and waiting for them to taste his dishes and offer their glowing praise, Zakariya could not stop checking his watch, anxious for his shift to end and the tables to clear out so he could hurry home to Jane. He took care of her needs from A to Z, and she yielded to all his pampering. She told him that no matter what happened, she would never go through pregnancy again because her body would not have the strength to withstand such a hostile attack a second time. He searched the internet, bought a book of advice for pregnant women, scheduled her meals and hours of sleep, did the ironing, checked her weight every other day, joined her on morning jogs in the park with all those oak trees as soon as she got over her morning sickness. Then he'd drive her to the OB/GYN clinic, make appointments for her there at times when he would be available to join her—the only man in a room full of women, to listen to the baby's heartbeat before the doctor confirmed to them after doing an ultrasound that Jane was having a girl.

"A girl!"

That was what Zakariya had been hoping for, despite hearing throughout his childhood nothing but everyone's desire to have boys. Lots of names of women from his family and their various qualities went through his mind. He now had a new treasure.

But married life wasn't always a long, happy river. In the fifth month, Jane went back to her horrible old ways. Zakariya came home one day after the lunch shift at the restaurant and didn't find her at home. Her phone was turned off. He didn't know where to look for her. He drank a lot of bourbon and sat in the dark in the living room waiting for her. Around midnight she came home drunk. He went berserk.

"Alcohol can kill the baby!"

"So, you care about me as long as I'm pregnant. After I give birth, you're going to give me the boot!"

Their shouting spilled out into the street. She wouldn't accept being chained down, refused to let anyone dictate how she should behave.

"I left home the day my parents yelled at me for coming home after midnight. I am free. Free with my time and my clothes and my friends!"

They stayed up until dawn. Zakariya understood that he must appease her and wait for the baby to be born. His biggest fear, his nightmare, was that she would take off with her. He made lots of cakes for her and delicious meals. He bought tickets to go see horse races; she loved horses and enjoyed seeing the hats worn by ladies in the VIP section. But she wouldn't stop running off to the nearest bar the moment dusk fell. She'd turned into a naughty child. Didn't keep her closet organized, didn't wash the dishes in the kitchen. At night, she took the liberty to sneak the cylinder out from under the bed where Zakariya usually kept it, open it up and pull out *The Blue Violinist*. And when Zakariya woke up after noticing she'd gotten out of bed, she asked him mockingly while pointing to the musician with the childlike face, "Is this our promised fortune?"

"In principle…Don't touch the painting with your fingers. You'll ruin it."

"Do you want me to show it to my friends?" she asked with a wink. "Maybe they can find a buyer."

"No way. Don't you dare do that. And don't mention anything about it to anyone. We might expose ourselves to robbery or murder. It's worth a lot. A *lot*."

The next day, and because he didn't trust Jane, he rented a safe deposit box at Saratoga Springs Bank without telling her and used it to put his mind at ease about the Chagall painting. He also realized as he was hiding Emily's diary in there too that he'd been distracted from the pain of losing his mother. Her sad memory would only descend upon him if he suffered a bout of insomnia. He had been distracted from his family by the joy of waiting for Mary's birth.

"Mary."

Their choice for the baby's name came to them without discussion. One day Jane called to Zakariya, "Don't you want to hear Mary's kicks?"

He put his ear over her belly and smiled in agreement.

"Mary is in a hurry to come out!"

That had been the easiest way to name a child. Jane remembered that she had wished for a baby in front of the Cathedral of the Virgin Mary in Strasbourg, and Zakariya liked the name after giving up on the idea of recycling family names. The new should be new. But labor was difficult and lasted for hours. Zakariya went with Jane to the hospital and when he got there, he suddenly started having pains at the base of his stomach that he had never experienced in his life. When he described the pain to the doctor, he told Zakariya it was just like labor pains and escorted him into the delivery room to support his wife. And there in the delivery room his pains went away as Mary came out and produced her first cries of life.

———————

Zakariya asked for paternity leave so he could spend time with Mary from her very first day. While the mother transitioned to the home, he would jump out of bed to his feet whenever the little one cried out in hunger. He'd heat up the milk for her after Jane refused to breast feed her for anthropological reasons. "It's the closest thing to being an animal," she'd say.

That wasn't the end of it, for after giving birth Jane slid into a depression that she never came out of, even as Mary celebrated her first birthday. It was a failed attempt when Zakariya tried to gather his little family together for a party to which he invited a few friends and neighbors. Without meaning to, Jane dropped the cake decorated with a single candle as she was carrying it to the living room. The icing went everywhere, and upon seeing the deep misery that appeared on her face, one of the neighbors volunteered to clean up the floor, and the guests satisfied themselves with glasses of fruit juice while expressing their admiration for the little angel. They unanimously nominated her to do modeling for TV ads for diapers and baby formula—a venture that was sure to make her parents a fortune.

Meanwhile, Zakariya and Jane's life turned into a never-ending fight that could only be stopped with input from Mary who picked up her parents' tension like radar from the air inside the house and would let out screams that were more like distress calls. Zakariya's ability to pacify his wife had begun to wane. He was getting upset, too. He stayed late at the restaurant on purpose sometimes or left the house all of a sudden.

He'd slam the door and wander the streets until the thing he always feared would happen happened.

As he was setting a table for a group of friends celebrating a birthday for one of them, Jane called him on his cell phone and asked him to come right away because Mary was crying. An unusual cry and she didn't know how to quiet her down. She was going to call an ambulance. He arrived in less than half an hour. He did not like this scenario. He parked the GMC and got out. The house was quiet. No crying, no sound at all. He opened the door and went inside. He called out to Jane but got no answer. He went into Mary's room and found her asleep with the musical mobile—princesses and horses and dwarves—spinning over her head. Meaning Jane had left a short time ago. He found a letter she left for him in the crib.

> *I wasn't lying the day I told you that I am incapable of settling down and that I'm not a good person to get involved with, and you should have believed me. I am leaving you now and never coming back. So, I'll be the first woman to flee from you. You, whose escapades with women always ended with your running away, as you say. Don't let your ego be wounded. I don't think I'm mistreating you very much if I leave you with Mary and help you get rid of me and my difficult life and my secrets that are more like miserable fantasies. Have her all to yourself. It's your dream. Now you are the King of India, as my dad used to say before locking himself in his room. There are a lot of women in your life with beautiful names. Emily, you talk about her as if she is a mythical creature. I secretly read the sections in English in her diary, but then you hid the*

189

diary, I don't know why. I felt she was my soulmate. Philomena, the American with her heroic deeds. She was a special breed of man from what you told me. And now you have a new legend—Mary Mubarak. I know without your having to tell me that you want to take her back to your homeland with you. You won't find a place for me in your golden book of women. I am Jane Malloy, daughter of a steel worker, who will not make a nest. I don't eat until hunger bites me, I get by on fast food and cheap hotels, a few cigarettes, and some songs. Don't try to get hold of me. I'm going to throw my cell phone over the first bridge I cross and I'm not going to get another one. I'm not going to chase after my mother. She went after her freedom late, so let it be. I hope that no one will come looking for me.

Calamity Jane

As it turned out, Jane wrote better than she spoke. He was relieved. He breathed a heavy sigh because she was gone, and she'd left the baby behind. He could not believe that he was living that moment, standing over Mary's crib, looking at her rosy cheeks, and not knowing what he was going to do when she woke up crying in a little while. He couldn't believe how happy he was. His life was wide open, and his gold was right there before his eyes. But Jane's goodbye letter and exit from his life revived in him the memories of an entire year of passion. And perhaps owing to the memory of his love for her, the next day he did what husbands do. He went to the city police station to report Jane missing. He didn't mention her letter, so they wouldn't consider her to have fled of her own free will, and he didn't point out that she'd left many of her belongings at the house either. He was told that there would not be any investigation into her absence before three days' time because she might come back. That was what statistics showed concerning missing persons reports. More than half of them came back within forty-eight hours, or she will have left by her free will. The policewoman ended up her explanation with a brief lesson for the foreigner.

"It's a free country, you know."

Finally, she gave him a missing person's report form to fill out. When he got to the question about "Special Characteristics," he wrote: "Very beautiful. Looks like Vivien Leigh."

17

The four years he spent with Mary were the most beautiful days of his life. He would lift her up near his nose and take a whiff to find out if she'd soiled her diapers. He'd proceed to clean her bottom with moist wipes, put on a new diaper, and kiss her legs. Her cheerful mood would return. She'd clap and cry out joyfully. He'd try to make his voice higher, serenading her with songs by Asmahan who, as his mother Emily used to say, after her and Umm Kulthum no other woman should ever be allowed to sing. He'd whisper in her ear, "*Layaali el-Unsi fi Vienna…* Oh Amorous Nights in Vienna…," he'd read her the poem "*Khaffa al-Qatin…*The Neighbors have Departed" by Al-Akhtal from the book '*Uyoun al-Shi'r al-'Arabi…*The Best of Arabic Poetry. He wanted her to be in tune with her mother tongue early. He'd tell her things as if speaking to an educated adult, like the myth of Astarte and Adonis and the red flowers that covered Mahmoudiya Orchard just before Good Friday every spring, and she would grab his nose and pull off his reading glasses while he showed her the colorful wooden blocks and the little toy elephants and giraffes and donkeys. He burped her after she drank her bottle, wrapped her in a baby carrier on his chest, and took her shopping and to the park. He'd help her stand up on her feet and take a step or two, then let her fall down and get back up again. He took pictures of her with his cell phone nonstop.

He wanted to capture her every emotion and every expression and all the colors of her dresses and baby rompers, or he'd take pictures of her naked as he dipped her into the bath water, then pulled her out crying and laughing. She'd fall asleep to the music of her wind-up carousel, and then when she woke him up with her first bout of nightly crying, he'd take her into his bed and she'd kick him and tumble onto him until morning when he'd get up gingerly and joyfully as though he were holding the whole world in his arms, to wait for the girl to come who would look after her while he was away preparing food at the restaurant.

The first year, he'd shared Mary with Jane, and the second year, he shared her with Clarita.

Clarita's sister, who worked as a waitress at The White Elephant, recommended her. When she arrived, he had made a list of tasks for her and stuck it to the refrigerator: At 11:00 encourage Mary to go potty; feed her the poached vegetables at noon and set up the mosquito net over her at naptime so the bugs won't feast on her tender skin. He excused Clarita from cooking for him and ironing his clothes—he liked to iron his clothes himself—so she could give her full attention to Mary. He laid down one rule, which was that she was not to take Mary out of the house no matter what. And she should call him the moment there was any emergency.

She was an undocumented immigrant from Mexico, kind in that rare way when kindness and deprivation coexist. He was generous with her, giving her tips on top of her weekly salary and all sorts of presents because his very soul was in her hands from nine o'clock in the morning until sundown. Clarita had a strong connection to Mary. She played with her all day, taught her to say things in Spanish to surprise her father with when he came home.

Zakariya would dismiss the babysitter the moment he got home so he could be all alone with Mary. Tied down by the daily routine, he kept postponing his plans to return to Lebanon. He was afraid to let his intimate bubble in Saratoga burst. He'd say he was going back and then do nothing to start planning. He didn't even tell his sister Marta that he had a little daughter with whom he was spending all of his time. The downtown did not beckon to him, he had no desire to go there looking for friendships or coffee shops. His world had been complete first with Jane. Jane, who didn't come home and didn't make a single attempt to get in touch, not by letter or by phone, as if announcing herself would cause a crack in the wall of her separation and send her reeling back home. He got worried about her once when Clarita told him that a woman had come knocking at the door, but she didn't open it in compliance with Zakariya's rules. From the description, he doubted it had been Jane coming back home to take Mary and run off with her.

In France, he had been a boring playboy; even Mathilde Lagrange didn't leave him with a deep wound. On this side of the ocean, he'd become compassionate and faithful, a willing prisoner to those he loved. After Jane, his world became complete with Mary. Mary was his toy. He'd put a ponytail in her hair, pick out shoes for her, make her dance to songs. She'd sit in the back in her car seat, and he'd drive her to hearing check-ups and vision check-ups and to get vaccinated and for urine labs. He worried there might be some imperfection in her, but they didn't find anything wrong. The doctor asked him about her mother, so he told him that he was raising her on his own. He strongly encouraged him to send her to nursery school.

"She needs more than just you!"

When she was three, he shared her with the Children's Garden. Zakariya cried the first day. She cried and he cried. Then he asked if he could stay with her until she got distracted from him or took a nap, so he could slip out and linger for a while behind the window to watch her and see how she would forget him and start making new friendships with her playmates sitting on the floor. She'd come home to him in the afternoon with English words she'd learned and crayon drawings. The day-care teacher told him that for the first several days, Mary made drawings of her father and no other subject but him. He'd take her on Sundays to see the camel and feed the giraffe and ride the horse at the zoo. Then he tried to make plans for his future life. He decided to let Mary go to school in Saratoga, and as soon as she finished her second school year they would embark on their big return to Tel Safra.

When she was five years old and had already learned a bit of English, Arabic, and Spanish, he sent her to first grade at a school with buildings that had red tiled roofs and were scattered around a natural wooded area. It offered all school levels, K-12. He would wait for the bus with her every morning and would be standing at the front door to the house when she came back at sunset. One time she asked him, "Where is my mother?" Her girlfriends had asked her why she didn't have a mother like they did. He told her that she had gone away, and he promised her that she would come back one day. He showed her as proof all the clothes and shoes that she'd left in the closet. Mary went along with it, but wasn't totally satisfied.

***

The days went by smoothly and happily. Until the doors of hell burst open.

Zakariya tried later on to no avail to remember what he had been doing at the restaurant, who had been standing beside him, and what he had been preparing for the daily special when he saw a "Breaking News" report on TV given by a police spokeswoman: "A shooting at West Lake School in Saratoga Springs."

"That's where Mary is!"

He didn't even remove his apron, didn't talk to anyone. He got into the GMC and flew to the school. The police had arrived. They'd blocked the entrance and cordoned off the area. They had gotten the shooter under control. But the search was ongoing for potential accomplices, and it was necessary to take every precaution.

***

Stanley Jackson Jr. lived with his mother—an alcoholic divorcee who'd drunk whiskey in excess during her pregnancy with him. He spent most of his day alone in his room listening to loud music and watching violent movies in which tough guy heroes vanquished bad guys of all sorts of weird races and colors, who fell like mosquitoes under their bullets and blows. He chatted on a website online with groups that secretly adopted the swastika as their logo and believed that the world would end soon, when the white race in America lost control. He stole money from his mother to buy weapons, and in a matter of two months easily gained possession of three automatic rifles and several boxes of ammunition. He informed his virtual friends that he was going to do something that would rock the whole world. They encouraged him to do whatever it was he was planning without asking for more details.

He parked his car by the wall of his former school on the back side of the building, picked up his bag of weapons and ammunition, and climbed over the wall. He knew West Lake School very well. He hid in a thicket of elm trees that he used to sneak off to when he was in high school to smoke pot when the recess supervisor wasn't paying attention. He readied his weapons, waited for the children to come out to the schoolyard, and started aiming at their heads.

Zakariya tried to go inside. He screamed, begged, and sobbed while repeating, "Mary, Mary" in an incessant delirium. He was the first of the children's parents to arrive and the last to leave. People came crowding in after him, while the shooting inside the school had ceased and a SWAT team climbed the walls from various locations. The door suddenly opened and out came a group of frantic children amid screams and hysterical crying, some of whom found their parents waiting for them and others who were escorted away from the school by the police. Zakariya was counting the children as they came out and scrutinizing them one by one; he didn't see Mary among them. He tried to go inside with another man amid the commotion, but the police barred them on the pretext of potential risk.

Stanley Jackson started firing single bullets at the children who'd come rushing out of class. Some fell and the rest fled back into the building following their teachers' orders. But Mary

Mubarak, as was written on the card stuck to her chest, ran in the opposite direction with her blond ponytails swinging right and left. One of the teachers spotted her. She called out to her, but Mary couldn't hear amid all the noise and confusion. She was wearing her little backpack with the water bottle, chocolate chip cookies, and crayons inside it. She ran in the direction of the elm thicket, toward Stanley Jackson Jr. who didn't even bother to take aim, picking her off at a distance of ten meters with a single bullet.

When panic set in and the children tried to get out of the line of his gunfire, he started shooting nonstop, switching from one machine gun to another until he ran out of bullets. Then he came out from hiding, stood there with his hands up, beside the dead and wounded children lying on the ground, and when the police approached him, barking their belated orders at him, and arrested him, he had that idiotic smile on his face, a preview to the eventual claim that he was mentally disturbed, which, without a doubt, he was. Years earlier, the New York Supreme Court had struck down the death penalty in the state.

The eight who were killed and fifteen who were wounded were taken to the nearest hospital. Gathered in the lobby were all the parents whose children hadn't come out of the school, all clinging to the one hope that their children's injuries hadn't been fatal.

Zakariya was staggering like a drunk, saying Mary's name, asking for her and getting no response. He was asked to sit down and told to wait for them to bring details, and then the nurse would disappear. They were avoiding him, but he didn't know that.

Then a young Asian doctor came out into the waiting room and called for the family of Mary Mubarak. The doctor was tearful. Zakariya stood up on his feet and collapsed onto the floor. "He lost his daughter," the doctor said and asked the medics to lift him onto a stretcher. He was given sedatives and when he regained consciousness, he said he had been telling Mary a story about a faraway town there in the East, about the prince's daughter whose lover kidnapped her on a flying carpet, and he wanted to see Mary so he could finish the story. That was all. The nurse covered her face and rushed out of the room.

They asked for his name and address and telephone number. They started deliberating among themselves and whispering back and forth, all coming to the same conclusion: he should not be allowed to see her. The psychological assistant explained to him that it would be better to remember her the way she was before what happened to her. Zakariya reflected, was persuaded, agreed, and hit his head against the wall so hard that it shook the wall of the hospital waiting room. Then he got up and headed to the exit door, tearing his summer hat apart with his hands and his teeth.

—

One of the neighbors who'd read the names of the victims went to Zakariya's house to wait for him at the front door, so he would be there for him when he arrived. The neighbor was a stout dark man of Indian origin. He hugged Zakariya and went with him into the house, where they sat in the living room in silence. Zakariya stood up from time to time, walked toward the front door, opened it, and went out to the street to gaze at the house before coming back inside, locking the door, and heading to Mary's room. He'd stand in front of her door, unable to bring himself to open it, and then go back to sit with his neighbor.

Eventually, Zakariya realized that he could not stay in the house by himself, so he asked his Indian friend to stay up with him out on the porch, which they did. After a long period of silence and another dose of sedatives, Zakariya told his neighbor that he had been planning to return to Lebanon with his daughter. But now he didn't know what to do. It was the only time the neighbor spoke.

"We Hindus burn our dead. The fire takes their souls and unites them with the heavenly beings and their ashes remain with us as a memory. Put your daughter's ashes in a bottle and take her with you wherever you want, to your country. I brought my mother with me from New Delhi, and she is still here on a shelf between my books."

———

And that was what Zakariya did. He left the house the next morning after thanking his neighbor a lot for consoling him and spent the remainder of his days in Saratoga Springs at a little hotel drinking whiskey, until he passed out. Sometimes he would drive over to the house and then go away again, repeating his attempts to see Mary. On one of those trips, he saw Clarita, the young babysitter, sitting at the front doorstep, covering her face as she sobbed. He got out and called to her from a distance, at first, not daring to go any closer. But then he went over to her and hugged her, asking her to pray for Mary in Spanish, to pray to the Virgin, after whom she had been named.

His Indian neighbor joined him at the solemn funeral mass for the school victims. The governor and some members of the state legislature were in attendance. Zakariya's hand trembled as he, along with the rest of the victims' family members, released a dove into the sky. And again his hand trembled as he signed the request to have Mary cremated, while overcome with tears and bitterness.

Jane Malloy did not come. She heard her daughter had been killed. She settled for sending a letter to Zakariya in which she said she would not attend Mary's funeral because she was incapable of it. And in any case, she was not going to last much longer in this life. "They're sending me to a mental asylum, but I won't let them. I have many ways to slip through their fingers," she wrote.

Her only request was to know where Mary was buried. And she had one last wish to visit her father again in Boston so she could sit with him in silence, gaze at his face, and leave for good after that.

Zakariya replied to her that he was going back to his country. He asked her to come to the house and do whatever she liked because he was never going back inside it again.

He didn't say goodbye to anyone except his neighbor. He asked him to go to the house and bring him Mary's toys. They hugged a long time. The neighbor gave him a gilded Mantra figurine with eight arms for protection before he headed to the bank and left carrying *The Blue Violinist*, Emily's diary, and Mary's ashes. He flew to Paris where he spent some time before returning to Tel Safra for good.

———

There was no trace of Zakariya Mubarak's stop in Saratoga Springs except an abbreviated report left in the Department of Social Services office, which maybe no one read or would ever read. It was signed by Adam J. Moritz, Psychological Assistant. He'd done a university research paper on the stereotypical behavior of victims of violence and their relatives. He had come back to interview Zakariya more than once at his hotel room. In the article he said:

Mr. Mubarak is in an advanced state of depression brought on by his strong attachment to his daughter, to whom he was both father and mother, and who was his whole world.

The psychological assistant did not put a lot of faith in the possibility that Zakariya could restore his mental state. Rather, he personally feared that Zakariya might venture into committing *"an act with dire consequences."*

18

Zakariya Mubarak's murder would not have gained much attention in the Lebanese media if the initial theory that the motive was related to a family inheritance dispute had stuck. When it first happened, the Beirut newspapers didn't give it more than a small box on the Miscellaneous News page, ending with the customary phrase, "And an investigation into the details of the crime is underway."

All mention of the incident quickly disappeared from the newspapers and print media, and started appearing in tweets from Twitter accounts whose owners signed with fake names such as "Mountain Saint," or "I love you, my homeland," or with their initials. They all bemoaned the hypocrisy of double standards. "If the murderer was switched with the victim and the victim with the murderer in the Tel Safra crime, it would have been solved with lightning speed." Or, putting it more concisely, "We get murdered, and no one even bothers to investigate."

It was obvious that the unnamed subjects mentioned here were none other than the Christians, since those accusations were marked with the hashtag #JusticeforZakariyaMubarak. And it became clear that the partisan lawyer who had secured the right-of-way to Mahmoudiya Orchard for the Mubarak family was the one behind this campaign that elicited numerous reactions, also from anonymous accounts assumed to belong to people of the Druze sect who framed the crime in the context of a history of actions and reactions. They reminded everyone that previous crimes had been committed and had gone unpunished—an allusion to Nassif Hamdan, who'd died after being shot and losing his leg decades earlier. Similarly, some went back to pointing the finger at "others" who collaborated with the enemy during the Israeli invasion of Lebanon. And some went way back into the past, all the way to the massacres of 1860. The reverberations reached Tel Safra, resurrecting ghosts from a bitter past that many of the townspeople had been glad to have successfully tucked away.

In the face of this civil war playing out on Twitter, the Ministry of Justice issued a statement asserting the integrity and impartiality of the courts, and warned against questioning the justice system, especially since the arrows of accusation had also reached Kamal Abu Khalid who had been mentioned deceptively on a Facebook page, saying that the appointed assistant investigating judge should not be a member of the same sect as the perpetrators of the crime, in a hasty claim that the Assistant Investigating Judge for Mount Lebanon belonged to the Druze sect. In reality, Kamal Abu Khalid, who was born in the mixed Ras Beirut neighborhood was registered in the Census Log as a

Syriac Catholic, a religious denomination that is a tiny minority in Lebanon, with two or three churches at most. His mother was a Palestinian Muslim whose family came to Lebanon on the heels of the 1948 Nakba.

Kamal Abu Khalid requested a meeting with the public prosecutor of the Mount Lebanon district. The public prosecutor commended Abu Khalid's merits and implored him to finish with the case, which the politicians might exploit as a means of settling their sectarian differences. Abu Khalid told him that he was very close to concluding the investigation and formulating his presumptive ruling, and that all the evidence pointed to the likelihood they were dealing with a case of suicide. All that remained was the ballistics report to confirm the corroborating evidence. The public prosecutor phoned the appellate prosecutor, who in turn reassured the minister of justice in regard to the expected conclusion concerning the death of Zakariya Mubarak.

———

Colonel Moussa, who was in charge of the newly established Central Crime Lab, whose inauguration was attended by the prime minister himself, had promised the investigating judge to have the results within three days of receiving the Glock 17, because there was some equipment they had yet to receive and thus were obliged to coordinate with a lab at one of the private universities to verify the results of the requested analysis. When the security officer sent by the investigating judge came in carrying the gun with his bare hands, Colonel Moussa screamed at him for mishandling a murder weapon, and then immediately called Kamal Abu Khalid. The colonel told Abu Khalid that it was impossible now to lift fingerprints from the gun, which had been passed from hand to hand among the gun dealers after being used to commit the Tel Safra crime. And he sarcastically added that he might find prints from both the victim and the murder suspect on the same gun.

Upon one final perusal of the case file, the investigator discovered that the name Gibran Younis Mubarak showed up again in a handwritten report that had come in shortly after the crime, stating that Gibran—the same man who'd been a prime suspect immediately following Zakariya's murder—had a long criminal record: convictions for forming a theft ring on Dock 5 at the Port of Beirut, accessory to murder, assaulting police officers in the line of duty. All of the convictions were pardoned by the general amnesty law that was passed by the Lebanese parliament following heated discussions that took place at the end of the civil war.

This sparked an idea in Abu Khalid's mind. The details led him back to Badih Makhlouf. He called him to come back immediately to his office.

"You are involved in this case!"

Makhlouf defended his innocence and started rehashing his life story, so the investigator interrupted him.

"Do you know a man by the name of Gibran Younis Mubarak?"

"Yes," he answered without hesitation. "I know him from our war days. He was young and eager to go into battle."

"Did you know he is Zakariya Mubarak's cousin?"

"No."

"Did you ever sell him a gun?"

"Yes."

"What model?"

"A Glock 17 too."

Kamal Abu Khalid felt he must certainly be in a bad dream.

"When was that?"

"Six months ago, when I received a shipment of new guns."

The investigating judge nearly regretted that the days of applying torture to get confessions out of suspects were over.

He let Makhlouf go, who couldn't understand why the investigator didn't charge him with the illegal gun sales he'd confessed to right there in his office.

Abu Khalid called in two of his assistants to take one last trip to Tel Safra before finishing with the whole mess. He'd grown certain, despite some contradictory signs, that the conclusion was drawing near. Having regained some feelings of confidence and relief, he exchanged some funny anecdotes with his companions on the road about the gold buried in the ground at the house they were headed to. One of the assistants told a similar story about a big cattle merchant who returned from Brazil and buried his fortune under his house in one of the villages in the Koura region of North Lebanon. Until today the house is still jointly owned by all the man's heirs. No one believes the gold is there, but no one dares forfeit his share of the property. Some of the cattle merchant's grandsons—one who settled in Stockholm and even one in Equatorial Guinea—still own fifty shares in their grandfather's "estate," as they call it boastfully.

Villagers have long sought riches that did not get eaten by time, especially during periods of economic decline. And how often did the people of Tel Safra themselves go digging for treasures and searching in books of magic, trying to find jewels and necklaces dating back to legendary kings. If only the investigating judge had widened his net of interviews, he would have discovered what people said about the Mubarak family and how the family had a book that they would read from to conjure spirits, and how from their houses they could hear strange sounds at night. And one would dare to tell him that their Aunt Raheel's tongue got knotted up and her mind got torn to pieces when the *jinns* hunted her down one time in the cellar of her house.

Kamal Abu Khalid and his assistants saw the eighty-year-old Raheel herself as soon as they entered the house. She was sitting on her couch holding a large pair of seamstress's scissors and cutting apart, with a shaky hand, a big piece of linen cloth that had a colorful design along the top. Immediately realizing what was happening, Abu Khalid rushed to take the scissors from her hand. Indeed, when he went closer to the painting, he found the peasant musician on it and the violin and the blotch of blue color. Raheel had already succeeded in cutting out the first bird standing on the man's shoulder and was now starting to cut out the white sun on the left side of the picture. Marta came in.

"What is happening here?" the investigator asked.

She tried to feign ignorance.

"You've known everything from the start."

"I'll tell you, but you won't believe me."

"Where did you find that painting? Do you know how much it's worth?"

"A young man I don't know came by yesterday saying my brother had a valuable painting that he wanted to buy."

If there was any special characteristic about Marta Mubarak, the house's final caretaker, it was that she rarely answered a question directly and instead embarked on some tiresome and unexpected response.

"So why are you letting your aunt cut it up?"

"Zakariya had hidden the painting in our aunt's room, and I gave it to her to play with while I was busy..."

"How did you know it's a fake?"

She didn't answer. But after a little while she added:

"I found the painting depressing and we've had enough depression around here. So I told my aunt to cut it up so we can put an end to our bad luck."

The inspector gave a sarcastic grin and pulled out the key to Zakariya's room from his pocket so he could go in one more time by himself. He was gone for ten minutes while Marta served coffee to his assistants and tried to calm Raheel down as she demanded to have *The Blue Violinist* back.

Kamal Abu Khalid came out frowning.

"How did you get inside Zakariya's room?"

"I didn't."

"You've had a duplicate key all along. Don't lie."

She burst into tears.

"He's my brother. I was carrying out his wishes!"

"Where's the bottle with the name Mary written on it?"

She choked on her tears without answering.

Kamal Abu Khalid reverted to using the element of surprise.

"Zakariya committed suicide. He shot himself."

She jumped back as though she'd been stung.

"He was planning to grow grapes and produce white wine from our orchard, and I was trying to find him a wife and was lucky to find one that I suggested to him. And he didn't say no."

Kamal Abu Khalid said goodbye to her, hoping never to see her again, and went to the church endowment agent to confirm his suspicions once again. The agent told him how Zakariya had had the family tomb renovated, and how his sister Marta had come to him to say that she did not want her cousins to be buried with them, because it wasn't right for the murderer and the victim to be buried side by side. Then she gave him a bottle she said contained the ashes of Zakariya's daughter, whose name was Mary, and asked him to bury her with him. So, he opened the door to the tomb and placed it beside Zakariya's coffin.

Abu Khalid tried to quarrel with him.

"And where do you stand concerning the resurrection of the body?"

"Many people bury things that are dear to them with their relatives…"

The investigating judge finished up his rounds in Tel Safra with a trip to the crime scene with his assistants, escorted by the driver of the jeep from the town police station. The sky was clear, and visibility was excellent. He thought it truly was a beautiful place to die, as the young woman from the Ancient Paths Club had said. The investigator asked the policeman if anyone from the station had come back there. He said no. He repeated the question, and he said no again.

They wandered around the place. Kamal Abu Khalid scrutinized every spot. His two assistants copied him, and one of them found a black notebook behind the trunk of a crab apple tree. He gave it to the investigator who opened to the first page to read: "The Diary of Emily Tabet Mubarak." He flipped through a few pages and then tucked it into his pocket. He wouldn't read it now for fear of finding more leads.

Kamal Abu Khalid left Tel Safra and headed down to Beirut thinking about how to word the presumptive ruling. He wanted to give it a literary flare, the way some clever judges known for their mastery of the Arabic language permitted themselves to do. He sought inspiration for his introduction from the metaphor of the geological fault line—atop which Tel Safra was said to be sitting, and that the Roman temple there hadn't been obliterated by the passage of time but rather had been destroyed by an earth-quake, possibly the same one that destroyed Beirut. And he would finish up by saying that Zakariya Mubarak was found dead at a dangerous crossroad where legends about gold and wars between brothers intermingled with the love of French women and the false promise of fortune, to an enmity that disappeared and re-awakened over the course of a century and a half, finding its way to a tragedy that moved from Saratoga Springs to Tel Safra. After that he would narrate in detail the story of the investigation. He'd meander into the strange personalities that created that case, most of whom were women, and also the confessions and coincidences that led the judge to the conclusion that Zakariya Mubarak had come back home to renovate the family tomb and die among his family, just as he had told the town's church endowment agent. He said he'd come back to die here, and he used for that purpose a gun, a Glock model…etc.

He was writing the introduction with great care, trying to create a logic and chronology for the facts on paper, to make up for the scrambling of factors and the tangling of the events in the investigation, when he received a call from Colonel Moussa, telling him he was on his way over to see him in person.

The colonel opened his briefcase and pulled out the report with a theatrical gesture. He placed it to the side of the investigator's desk without opening it and then pulled out the gun and the bullet and the empty cartridge. He spread them out before him before stating his findings.

"This bullet does not match this empty cartridge. And that's simple to confirm, because they're two different sizes. And the two don't match the gun, so all three pieces are from different sources. And in any case, the brand-new Glock 17 has never been used to fire any bullet because the barrel is still clean and unmarked."

Kamal Abu Khalid, who had remained standing to hear the colonel's findings, dropped with all his weight into the chair and started banging his pen on the top of his desk. That case was possessed. It was going to destroy him. He asked Colonel Moussa to sit down, too. A long silence prevailed upon them that was broken finally by the colonel.

"I asked them to rerun the analysis several times after getting that surprising result, and the findings always came back the same."

His presumptive ruling fell apart, turned into some sort of exercise in rhetoric. Abu Khalid had no idea how he was going to face the public prosecutor, and he no longer had the physical energy to resume the investigation, whose elements appeared to be liable to breed new offspring with no end. As far as asking to be taken off the case, that would be the worst solution. He was still young, he was an optimist, he was a prosecutor. He raised his head, looked at Colonel Moussa, remembering what he had overheard once that if he thought hard enough about some matter that he was requesting from someone and looked that person directly in the eye, then that person would get the message. He played the role of the self-assured man.

"Impossible! Everything came directly from the crime scene."

He would no longer allow such a lie to give him pause.

Colonel Moussa appeared to understand, especially since he wasn't confident about the testing tools or the people running the tests. The lab was still just getting started and some mistakes had already been made.

The investigating judge asked him with a frank smile, "Can you run the analysis one more time, for my sake?"

"Of course," the colonel said sympathetically and left the office.

Kamal Abu Khalid took out Emily's diary and started reading about that woman's struggles with the things of life, reaching all the way to the final page, which was written in a new handwriting and different ink. He realized quickly that it had been added by Zakariya Mubarak.

> I, who never wanted a child, gave in to that experience, and today I am in hell, trying to get out while a heavy iron chain pulls me down by the neck. But I want to live for the sake of my daughter Mary, so she will live on in someone's memory. If I am extinguished, her memory will be extinguished. Maybe here in my homeland I will find some reasons to keep going for her sake…

The world would turn one more time with the investigating judge in that field of puzzles before he shut the diary and shoved it into his desk drawer.

In the afternoon, Abu Khalid took his French bulldog out for a walk along the corniche, bracing himself to boost his spirits as he waited for relief to come the next day. His nervousness transferred to the dog who tugged on the leash and uncharacteristically pestered the other pedestrians.

Colonel Moussa did not delay in accomplishing the mission. At ten o'clock the next morning he sent a sealed report marked, "Highly Sensitive" with a security officer on bicycle and asked him to deliver it by hand, addressed to the Assistant Investigating Judge for Mount Lebanon.

Kamal Abu Khalid read the revised summary of the analysis, which said that the bullet that was found in the vicinity of the victim after having pierced through his body was indeed fired from the Glock 17. He began formulating the presumptive ruling in preparation for submitting it the next day to the public prosecutor, with the recommendation to halt the investigation and seal the case file.

The following week, he bought a watch equal in price to the Glock 17 on the black market in Beirut and sent it as a gift to Colonel Moussa, while telling himself apologetically, "*This death will be the least harmful, and least complicated.*"

Translator's Note

The King of India and Douaihy's novel *Printed in Beirut* have sometimes been referred to as mystery or crime fiction, since they do indeed share many elements associated with that genre. Their popularity undoubtedly stems from their compelling plot lines. But in addition to hooking the reader into turning the pages and searching for clues, Douaihy delves into Lebanese society and history, and presents them with biting irony.

They are detective novels not only in that the reader is drawn into solving crimes, but also into uncovering hidden and unexpected life stories and events. And so, *The King of India* is inevitably laced with trauma narratives of the country. But Douaihy writes about these wounds with moral imagination, giving readers the distance needed to be able to process what is being narrated without being swamped by it, a distance achieved through compassionate clarity of observation and luminous prose. *The King of India* absorbs our attention as a murder mystery, but one that also manages to escape from its own genre, rising to a graceful elegy for lost souls—a crime victim and the homeland that he can never forget.

About the Author

Jabbour Douaihy (1949–2021) was a novelist, teacher, generous mentor, and lucid chronicler of his cherished homeland of Lebanon. His works include *Autumn Equinox*, *Rayya of the River*, *The Spirit of the Forest*, *Rose Fountain Motel*, *June Rain*, *Chased Away*, *The American Quarter*, and *Printed in Beirut*. Douaihy has been nominated four times for the International Prize for Arabic Fiction, the region's most celebrated literary award. His 2001 novel for young readers, *The Spirit of the Forest*, published in French, received the Saint-Exupéry award. *Poison in the Air*, his last work, a cautionary tale on the dangers of listening only to our own voices, will be published by Interlink, in a translation by Paula Haydar.

About the Translator

Paula Haydar is assistant professor of Arabic at the University of Arkansas, where she earned her MFA in literary translation and PhD in comparative literature. She is the translator of fifteen contemporary Arabic novels, including five by Jabbour Douaihy. Her translations have won prestigious awards, such as the highly commended runner-up of the 2014 Saif-Ghobash Banipal Prize for Arabic Literary Translation, the 2011 Three Percent Best Translated Book Awards, the 1996 Arkansas Arabic Translation Award, and a National Endowment for the Arts grant.